KATHARINE'S YESTERDAY

YESTERDAY

AND OTHER STORIES

*Also by Grace Livingston Hill
in Large Print:*

The Honeymoon House and Other Stories
Lo, Michael
The Mystery of Mary
The Obsession of Victoria Gracen
Patricia
Re-Creations
Where Two Ways Met
By Way of the Silverthorns
The Christmas Bride
Ariel Custer
Head of the House

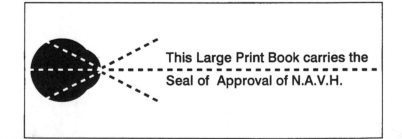

KATHARINE'S YESTERDAY

AND OTHER STORIES

Grace Livingston Hill

Thorndike Press • Thorndike, Maine

This Thorndike Large Print edition by Grace Livingston Hill is a combination of two books previously published by Tyndale House Publishers entitled *Katharine's Yesterday* and *The Love Gift*.

Printing History
"Katharine's Yesterday," "An Excuse for Christ," "John Chamberlain's Easter Coat," "A Voice Unheard," "The Pledge," "A Missionary Meeting," "Some Carols for the Lord," and "The Praise of Men," were originally published by Lothrop Publishing Company in 1895.

Published in 1998 by arrangement with Munce Publishing.

Thorndike Large Print ® Candlelight Series.

The tree indicium is a trademark of Thorndike Press.

The text of this Large Print edition is unabridged.
Other aspects of the book may vary from the original edition.

Set in 16 pt. Plantin by Minnie B. Raven.

Printed in the United States on permanent paper.

Library of Congress Cataloging in Publication Data

Hill, Grace Livingston, 1865–1947
    Katharine's yesterday, and other stories /
Grace Livingston Hill.
        p.   (large print)   cm.
      ISBN 0-7862-1649-2 (lg. print : hc : alk. paper)
      1. Christian fiction, American.   2. Large type books.
I. Title.
[PS3557.O839K37   1998]
    813'.54—dc21   98-40404

Contents

Contents

Katharine's Yesterday

Katharine Bowman stood at the front gate of her father's house, looking drearily down the road at nothing in particular. The air was crisp and clear, and the sunshine of the early morning was making everything dance and sparkle. All the brilliant red leaves, with their dew-covered faces, came fluttering down with a frosty air. They clanked and clattered against one another, as if to pretend that fall was well on its way and winter would soon be here. Nothing could have looked more enticing that October morning; the air, the sunshine, the leaves, and the very grass seemed full of delightful possibilities. Katharine saw them all: the little whirls of white dust down the road; the purple and blue mists on the distant hills at the end of the street; the big hill, or "mountain" as it was called, which loomed up before her just across the meadows. She had climbed it in company with a party of young people only a few days before. A

7

little brisk black-and-tan dog moved along the sidewalk in a lively manner, and the cheerful little sparrows that hopped in the road did not care whether winter came or not, but none of them gave Katharine any pleasure or sense of joy.

The truth was, the world looked pretty dark to her that morning. She had just come from the depot, where she had watched the morning express whizz out of sight, carrying with it half a dozen young people, who had been all in all to her the whole summer. They had played tennis and croquet together, had read and sung, walked and talked, gone on picnics, taken rides, and, in short, done all the delightful things that a party of congenial, bright young people can think up to do during a long summer in a country village.

The last delegation of them had gone away this morning; and now only Katharine was left, surrounded by all the pleasant places where they had enjoyed themselves together. How dreary they looked to her now. What was that great hill now, with its waving scarlet foliage and its stores of autumn brilliance? Nothing but a hill, which she would not climb alone. What was the tennis court, with its clean-shaven smoothness and its clear, white lines, over which played the mirthful sunshine and occasionally a yellow-and-brown leaf? Nothing but a desolate reminder of happy days all gone.

Yes, the summer was over and the winter had begun, a whole long winter, full of work and disagreeableness. She remembered the old brown cashmere dress that lay on her table this morning. Her mother had put it there, reminding her that it should be ripped, sponged, and pressed, to be made over. How she hated made-over things! She glanced down at the stylish street suit she had on. It would have to be put away and kept only for special occasions, now that there was no more company. Her pretty tennis suit, too, would have no use. Then there was a pile of mending, that had been accumulating during the months when she had given herself over to good times. What else was there not to be done, day in and day out, this long, barren winter?

In the house a pile of dishes was awaiting her attention. The servant had gone away for a day or two, and Katharine knew that the dishes would be left until she returned from the station, as her mother was very busy with the dressmaker. Still she lingered at the gate, dreading to go in and begin the winter. She thought miserably of the other happy girls who had left her, some to spend their winters in boarding school, others in their city homes, and the young men, most of them in college or at their business. It must be so nice, she thought, to be in business, and not have to poke at home and wash dishes. She wished she could go to school this winter. Why was it that her father's business could not have been as good this particular winter, just when she would have so enjoyed going to the seminary with Mabel and Fannie?

She drew a long sigh, and turned away from the gate, drawing off her gloves as she moved slowly toward the house. She would not look at the tennis court as she passed it, and two tears slipped out and rolled down her cheeks. She did so love tennis, and now there would be no more until next summer. Of course, she could not play alone.

But once in the house there was plenty to be done, and no one else there seemed to have time to think of yesterday.

"Katharine, I wish you would wash the dishes as soon as possible, and then make a cake. Mrs. Whiting is coming down to tea tonight and to go to prayer meeting, and there isn't a bit of cake in the house. Make the easiest, quickest kind, and get through as soon as possible. There is a great deal to be done, and I shall need your help this morning." Her mother said this as she entered the door.

Yesterday, when Katharine had been playing tennis, Frank Warner, her partner, had watched her several times. He had thought what a pleasant expression she always had, and what an exceedingly nice girl she was, for a girl who had been brought up in a small village, and whose father had never been able to give her many advantages. But he would scarcely have known her if he could have seen her now as she took off her hat and jacket, with an almost sullen expression on her face, and her brows drawn together in an inartistic scowl.

There was no time for her to examine the package that the girls had given to her at parting, and which she had not had the heart to open before, so she laid it on the table to wait until a leisure moment should come.

It seemed to her as though the task of washing all those sticky, ugly looking dishes was an impossible one, and likely to prove interminable. She made it all the harder for herself by continually envisioning pleasant things that had happened the days before, and discontentedly wishing those days back once more.

The work of getting the dinner fell mostly upon her shoulders that day, and it was performed very reluctantly. She scowled at everything, and sighed until her brother John told her she sounded like a steam engine. She told him in reply that he was a saucy, unbrotherly fellow. Then she went to work to make a pudding for dinner which she knew he did not like, just because it took less time than others which he did like; and things did not matter to her much, anyway, that day. Her heart was all in the past summer, mourning for it and its joys as one does for a dead friend.

Dinner was over at last, and the dishes washed; but there was no rest nor leisure yet for Katharine. Indeed, she had so prolonged her work by glooming over it, that it was quite late in the afternoon before she went up to her little room and began slowly to smooth her hair. Her mother's voice called from the sewing room where she had been all day with the dressmaker. "Katharine, Mrs. Whiting has just turned the corner, and is coming this way. She has come down very early. You will have to go downstairs and receive and entertain her for a while until I can come. I am sorry, but I cannot possibly leave this work just now. Do the best you can, dear."

That was all; and then the door of the sewing room shut quickly, and the hurried mother went back to her work, while Katharine scowled harder than ever, and went slowly, crossly, down to the door to welcome old Mrs. Whiting. Her greeting was by no means cordial; and her mode of entertaining her was so stiff and disagreeable that the poor lady felt quite ill at ease, until at last the gentle mother came down, and Katharine was set free to attend to the supper.

"I shall not be able to go to prayer meeting tonight, daughter; I feel one of my nervous headaches coming on, and shall have to go to bed. You can go to the meeting with Mrs. Whiting, dear, can't you?"

This sentence, spoken at the tea table, with old Mrs. Whiting sitting opposite to her and listening, seemed to Katharine the climax of the ugly day. Of course there was nothing to be said but "Yes," when she was asked before everyone. She thought to herself as she went for her hat and jacket, "Is all the winter to be like this, I wonder? Oh, what a contrast to yesterday!"

Prayer meeting seemed the height of

dreariness to Katharine tonight. She was never at any time fond of going, and usually got out of it as often as she could. To think of having to sit in that dark little room, where all the lamps smoked and the air smelled strongly of kerosene, and listen to several long prayers and talks by some old men and women! She recoiled from the idea, and thought, as she had done a dozen times that day, of the evening before, and the merry party that had gathered at one of the pleasant homes in the village for a farewell frolic.

The meeting was not quite as dreary as she had pictured it. More were out than usual, and there was a spirit of earnestness in all that was said that would have surprised her if she had not been too much wrapped up in her morbid thoughts to pay any attention to what was going on. But the air was as full of kerosene and dust as she had expected, and she turned up her nose over it, and wished for the end of the meeting to come.

At last the day was over, and Katharine was seated in her room with the little package in her lap, and leisure to open it. She untied the strings slowly, thinking of the dear friends who had left it, wondering to herself why the summer could not have lasted longer, and why it was that a winter with its hard work must come.

DIFFERENCE

The package proved to be made up of several smaller ones. Each of the girls had remembered her with some little parting gift, and the several packages were characteristic of the donors. The first contained a dainty pair of kid gloves, well chosen for the one who was to wear them, and perfect in size, shape, and color. These were from Fannie, who enjoyed pretty clothes so much. Next, a small volume of essays from Mabel, the literary member of the company. From Frances, the needle-worker, a small sachet bag, elaborate in satins of delicate shades and exquisitely painted bolting cloth. It looked like Frances, and the faint, sweet odor of it reminded one of her. Then from Cousin Hetty, a blank book, bound in leather, with pockets in the covers, ample pages dated for each day of the year, and a lovely fountain pen with gold-banded cap. This was to be used as a diary, and to be written in every day, so said a note slipped inside the cover. "Keep log notes, you know, Kathie, as they do on ship-board, for us to read next summer when

15

we all come back. And you must put down your real thoughts too — your own original ones — so that we can live your winter over with you next year."

Katharine curled her lip as she finished reading this note, and her eyes were filled with that gloomy discontent which had shone so plainly all day upon her face. What was there for her to write that the girls would care to live over with her next summer? How would they stand it if they really had to live it with her, or in her place? It was easy enough for them to write pleasant things that happened, and make them interesting, too, with their lives full of boarding school and lectures and concerts, and all sorts of delightful occupations; but what was she to do? There would be nothing but dishes and ripped-up dresses and dismal prayer meetings for her to write about the whole long winter through. She sighed again as she looked at the pretty things in her lap.

But the treasures were so new and precious that she sat up to examine and enjoy them once more. The sachet bag was admired again, and finally placed in her handkerchief box, carefully guarded by her finest embroidered handkerchief. The gloves were tried on, and fitted perfectly;

the volume of essays was glanced into, and found to look really quite interesting. Then came the diary to be written in; for of course she must try the new pen immediately, and the book ought to be started, even if there wasn't anything to write about. She poised the pen in the air, and drew her forehead together in a thoughtful frown, and then after a few minutes dashed ahead, and began.

"I must write my thoughts in this book, they say," she wrote. "My thoughts for every day; but I have no thoughts that are pleasant to write today. My pleasant thoughts are all of yesterday. Oh, if it were back! If I could see the girls once more! If I could live the summer over again! It was so bright and happy! Yesterday the hill looked so lovely, the tennis court was so delightful; and now all have a lonely, don't-care look. I cannot see the use in a life that is all made up of washing dishes and going to poky prayer meetings. Such a life as Mrs. Whiting has! I wonder if I shall ever care for it when I get to be an old lady. It doesn't seem as if I could stand to be an old lady, anyway. Think of having to come down here to tea, where nobody wants her, in order to get any pleasure! Oh, it is awful! I wonder why people can't stay young always. I wish I was rich! I can't understand why everyone can't be rich. It wouldn't hurt anyone! I am just tired of having only one servant — and she has to go home every day or two to take care of some sick sister or other — and ripping up old dresses. I wish I never had to wear another made-over dress. I *hate* them!"

Under this word hate she made a black, crooked little flourish, and stopped a moment with a mark just like it puckered into her forehead, and her lips twisted into the shape of the word hate. Then she seemed to realize a little what sort of a spirit she had been showing all day, and what she had put upon the clear, white sheet before her; and she bent her head once more, and wrote: "Oh, how ugly I am, anyway! I wish I could be different; but I can't."

She put the cap on her pen, and with a long-drawn sigh placed it in its little case. But in opening the cover of the book she discovered a small slip of paper. She pulled it out, wondering if it were another note from Hetty. No; it was only a little printed card. The heading caught her eye — "Difference," in large letters. It seemed a queer title for anything. She read the first line:

I was poor yesterday, but not today.

She smiled half sneeringly to herself. That wasn't her case. She might be said to have been rich yesterday, but today there was nothing but drudgery and dismal prospects. She read on, to discover why the individual who wrote it was poor no longer.

I was poor yesterday, but not today;
For Jesus came this morning
And took the poor away;
And he left the legacy
He promised long ago.
So peace and joy and love
Through all my being flow.

A strange feeling took possession of her as she read the quaint little poem:

I was tired yesterday, but not today.
I could run and not be weary,
This blessed way;
For I have his strength to stay me,
With his might my feet are shod.
I can find my resting places
In the promises of God.

A servant yesterday, a child today,
A loved one of his household,
Bearing his name alway.
Do you know this blessed difference?

Do you long for this better way?
He will come to you as he came to me
With the joy of an endless day.

No, she did not know that difference, and she was not at all sure that she longed for that better way. Indeed, that way did not seem better to her, but it always seemed gloomy and forbidding.

It was the first time in her life that she had ever really taken into her consciousness the thought that there might be joy in the service of Christ for any but very old people who did not expect to live long anyway. There was a charm in the bit of rhyme that made her read it over again before she put it away. Was it really true that Jesus could take the "poor" and the "tired" away, and leave happiness? Had he promised a legacy to her? What was it? What were the promises of God, that made themselves into resting places? She was tired, and she wished she could feel that way, and stop thinking about yesterday. Somehow even that didn't look very bright now. There was an uplifting about the thoughts written here that for the moment helped her to realize the comparative smallness of all other joys. She put it away in the pocket, and went about her preparations for the night; but serious thoughts of a different kind from any she had ever had before kept coming and going in her mind. At last the light was turned out, and she knelt beside her bed, as was her custom, for the few formal words of prayer which she had said every night since she was old enough to lisp the words. There had never been any real heart praying in them. It had been a mere form, gone through without much thought, and more from habit and a superstitious feeling that something would go wrong if she omitted it, than from any desire to ask anything from the Father in heaven.

But tonight as she knelt, a new feeling came to her. She seemed to be coming into a strange, mysterious Presence which she had never known before. She had not doubted that there was a God, or that he heard prayer; but the question had never had enough thought from her to be even raised in her mind. Now she seemed suddenly brought face to face with a new idea. Was God standing near listening when she spoke? Did he care to hear, and would he answer? What was this feeling that had come over her? Was it possible that he was speaking to her? Her heart had been so desolate and lonely all day, she began to feel the need of something outside herself to make her happy. A sudden longing came over her to have this wonderful "difference" in herself, to know what it was to have Jesus come and take the self-weariness away, and make things bright for her. Half unbelieving that there was such a thing, or that Christ would or could give her a real joy, she followed a sudden impulse, and resolved to tell him all about it. "O Jesus Christ," she prayed, "I am so tired of myself! If there is any way to make me different, please do." She was not much used to praying, except in formal words, and so the words did not come freely; but she knelt long, her lips not framing any words, but her heart sending forth an earnest petition for something to satisfy the great longing in her heart.

She relighted the lamp again before she lay down, and took down her Bible that had been neglected much, opening at random, and beginning to read at the first place. It proved to be the eleventh chapter of Matthew. She read on without much taking in the meaning of the words, until she came to the last three verses: "Come unto me, all ye that labour and are heavy laden, and I will give you rest. Take my yoke upon you, and learn of me; for I am meek and lowly of heart: and ye shall find rest unto your souls. For my yoke is easy, and my burden is light." Of course the words were as familiar to her as they are to you and me; and yet, because of their familiarity, and because of the urgent need of her soul, they seemed to mean more to her that night than they ever had before.

She put away the book, thinking as she once more turned out her light and lay down, how very tired she was, and how much she would like to be rested. She wondered how Jesus Christ could rest her, and whether he would, and wished it would come soon. Then she closed her eyes, and thought of the past summer again, and of the girls. A slight smile crossed her face at thought of Cousin Hetty. Hetty would be glad if she could have seen her reading the Bible, she was sure. Hetty was a true Christian, if there ever was one; and then Katharine sighed, and thought how impossible it would be for her to ever be as good as Hetty was, and wished again she were rich, and did not have to do things she disliked.

The October wind sighed among the half-naked branches outside the window, and the distant sound of the whistle of the midnight train could be faintly heard, as Katharine dropped off to sleep.

FINDING REST

The next morning after breakfast, while she stood at the kitchen door waiting for some concoction on the stove to boil, Katharine thought over this matter of rest.

She was watching old Andy, the man who sawed wood for them, and wondering how he stood his cheerless life, full of hard work. Where did the rest come in for him? She resolved to ask him. He was fond of talking to Miss Katharine; and many a long sermon he had preached to her, choosing his own text. Sometimes he began:

"Ah, Miss Katharine, an' isn't this a bright, beauty morning, to be sure! Oh, how good our God is to make us such mornings! We just ought to be praisin' him all the day long. Sometimes I feel just like gettin' right down in the dust an' ashes an' a-tellin' him what a sinner I be for not bein' thankfuller for all his goodness to me."

Katharine liked to hear him talk. There was a quaint earnestness about him which always interested her, and sometimes his thoughts were original. She turned to him as he came near where she stood, to put the armful of wood he had just finished sawing on the neat pile he was constructing near the door.

"Andy," she said, more real earnestness in her voice than she was accustomed to use when speaking to the old man, "do you know that verse about 'Come unto me, all ye that labour and are heavy laden, and I will give you rest'?"

"Oh, certain, certain, miss; that I do!" responded Andy heartily, stopping in front of her, the great armful of wood clasped tight in his worn old arms. "Many's the time, miss, when I've come, weary an' heavy laden as I was, an' foun' that rest. Oh, it's wonderful! wonderful!" and he drew one hand meditatively across his eyes, then began to lay the sticks in regular rows on the pile.

"But, Andy," said Katharine, with a puzzled expression, "you have to work hard all the time just the same. I don't see as you've been given any rest."

"Surely, Miss Katharine, you didn't suppose I was never to work again, did you? The good book never says, 'Come unto me, all ye that labor an' are heavy laden, an' I will take away your work, so that you won't have to do it any more.' Why, that would be to make a lazy set of folks of us; an' Jesus himself, when he was here on the earth, he worked hard. No; oh, no, miss! Rest never means no more work. Why, when a man's rested he's all ready an' eager to work again, an' especially if the work's for the One who's rested him; an' I reckon all work that's right to do at all is for him. That's my way a-thinkin'. Ah, I've come to him many a time, an' he's made me all ready to go out an' go to work again. He's took the tiredness all away, an' made me new again. What would the Lord do with a lot o' laborers a-sittin' roun' on the edges o' the vineyard, a-foldin' their hands, and a-sayin', 'I'm gettin' rested'? Why, it don't take him no time at all to rest us! He can do it quick's we ask him, or quicker, too, for the matter o' that. It just 'pears to me that that there verse about restin' is the unlaziest verse in the hull Bible; 'cause if a man's got rest, what need's he of it? Course he'll go right to work."

Something was boiling over, and Katharine was obliged to go in and attend to it; and Andy went back to his saw again, humming in a quavering old voice:

"Work, for the night is coming,
When man works no more."

26

Katharine, as she stirred the boiling mixture on the stove, told herself she needed rest; for she certainly did not feel like working at anything, and wondered how she could get it. Instantly came the answer in the words of her text: "Come unto me, and *I* will give you rest."

But there was really very little time to think about that or anything else. The day was even fuller of duties than the one before. There was much nerve-trying ripping, work that had to be done carefully, just a little slip of knife or scissors should cut the goods. Besides, the dress she was ripping was for herself, and was one that she had never liked. To add to the disagreeableness of her task, there was no possibility of bettering the dress by having it made over in any very pleasing fashion; for everyone was wearing long, straight-up-and-down dresses, with little or no drapery, and this dress had been made with much half-length drapery, and all the breadths were hopelessly short. Katharine's temper was by no means smooth when she had finished her work and sat down to the dinner table with her father, mother, and brother.

Her brother was a little younger than herself, but tall for his age, and would easily pass for a year or two older than he was; but they were never much together. The truth was, there were many particularly trying things to Katharine about her brother. She often wondered why it was that he always had to act so shy and awkward, and almost disagreeable, whenever he went among people with her, and especially when there were summer guests in town. Besides, he smoked cigarettes — when he was out of his mother's sight — and always had the odor of the corner grocery about him. Katharine wished much that her brother were like some other girls' brothers, but never dreamed that she was in the least to blame for the sort of brother he was. Now, as she sat down to the table opposite him, with her nerves all unstrung over the utterly impossible task of planning a stylish suit out of the old brown cashmere, her eye fell upon the bright colors of her brother's new necktie, and it struck her as extremely loud and out of taste. It was a little thing, perhaps, to put one out of temper with one's brother; but the inharmony of the colors jarred her, and expressed in one flaring, tangible thought the whole idea of the difference between her brother and some other boys she knew. She fixed her eyes upon the offending bit of silk; and all the disappointment and ill-temper of the morning, and, indeed, of the day before, vented itself in some sharp words she said to John about his tie.

Now John was good-natured, and usually replied to any sharp words of his sister in bright, funny retorts, until father and mother would break down in a laugh, and the whole would end in merriment; but today his face clouded over, and the color rose in his cheeks. The truth was, he did not like the tie much himself. He had good taste, and knew as well as his sister when a thing was becoming. But he had wanted some money very much for some scheme of his, and this tie had been a little cheaper than the one he preferred, so on a sudden impulse he had bought it.

"If you don't like my tie, you needn't look at it!" he retorted in a gruff tone. "There are plenty of other directions to look. You get so set up with all your elegant young gentlemen here in the summer, you can't speak decently to your own brother anymore. I'd just like to have that snob of a Frank Warner see you now. He'd think you were a perfect angel." And he broke off his sentence with a rough laugh.

It was Katharine's turn to flash her eyes and grow red in the face now, and more sharp words came from her lips.

It was a very uncomfortable dinner. Of course the father checked John in the midst of his bitter reply to Katharine, and then administered a sharp rebuke to Katharine, which brought the red still deeper to her cheeks. John swallowed his dinner rapidly, declined any dessert, and then departed, while his mother looked after him with a weary, anxious face, and sighed; and the father, following her troubled glance, grew more severe of countenance, and said to Katharine, "If you would devote a little more of your time to your own brother, and less to other girls' brothers, he might turn out more to your liking."

Then Katharine left the table in a deluge of tears, and spent the rest of the afternoon in her own room, alternately blaming and pitying herself. The father and mother, left to enjoy their dinner alone, ate little, and sat for the most part in troubled silence, wondering what they had done or left undone in bringing up their children that they should turn out in such a disappointing way.

Already to Katharine the dreaded long winter seemed far on its way. It could not be, she thought, that it was only two days since the girls and boys had all been here.

Oh, if the winter were ended, and a new summer begun! She thought over the scene at the dinner table. How dreadful it was to have her father talk so to her about John! What could she have done? Anything? No; John was not like others. He did not care for anything she did. If he only did, what a comfort he might be! And she fell to picturing him as she would like to have him. But her thoughts ended in her feeling quite well satisfied with her own conduct, and very much dissatisfied with her brother. Still, she was unhappy. She thought often also during the afternoon of the "rest," and wished she knew exactly how to "come" in the right way, that she might be sure to get it. Nevertheless, when she prayed that night, though she asked to be shown how to come, she asked in a halfhearted way, and not at all as if it were the one great desire of her life. She looked back to the bright days of fun and frolic as even more desirable. She wrote much in her new diary that night about longing to have rest. She carefully recalled and noted down what Andy had said about it, and thought with satisfaction of the delight with which the girls would read this entry next summer; for she knew they would appreciate and enjoy Andy's quaintness as much as she had.

As she had read over what she had written, Satan, leaning over her shoulder, whispered in her ear that it sounded very well; and I am sure that if her good angel had not put the thought into her heart to take out the little poem once more and read it over, she would have gone to bed that night with too high an estimate of herself.

I can find my resting places
In the promises of God.

These two lines of the poem kept saying themselves over after she had lain down. What were some of the promises of God? She tried to think of one. "I will give you rest." The words seemed to speak themselves to her. She had not realized that this was a promise in which she could have sure confidence. She fell asleep with a feeling that she could and would find that rest somewhere.

THE ANSWER

It seemed a strange thing to Katharine that the next Sunday morning the minister should take for his text those very verses about which she had thought so much during the week. She looked up at him with startled eyes when he announced it, as though he must surely have been reading her thoughts. She had not wanted to go to church at all that morning. Indeed, she never was fond of going; and today it seemed lonely to go and miss the bright faces of her various friends. She had tried to think up a good excuse, but none was forthcoming, and so she went. She was not in the habit of giving much heed to the sermon, but this morning her attention was caught and fixed before she was aware of it; indeed, she scarcely took her eyes from the minister's face until he had finished.

He spoke forcibly and clearly about the way to "come"; dwelt for a few moments on the wonderful rest that God could give; but the main part of his sermon was about the thoughts in the last verse, "Take my yoke upon you, and learn of me." He made it appear that it was the duty of everyone who had come to Christ to take his yoke. Then he told how a yoke was something to make work easier, and that Christ's putting this sentence right after the other one about coming to him, showed that he wanted and expected everyone who came to him to go to work immediately. Some yokes were made for two, he said, with one end heavier than the other. Christ's yoke was like this and he would work with us and bear the heavy end of the yoke, so that our work might not be too great for our strength. That work could not help but be easy and beautiful with Jesus Christ to help and to go with us, wearing the same yoke. He closed with the words, "For my yoke is easy, and my burden is light." And Katharine felt that she had never known what those words meant before.

It was a simple sermon, perhaps might have been called commonplace by some; but either Katharine's eyes were getting opened to see new things in the words of truth, or else she had never listened before, for she thought it a wonderful sermon. She looked about on the congregation when it was finished, and felt surprised to find Deacon Ewing yawning, and Mrs. Moffat evidently awaking from a refreshing nap, while her brother John's eyes were just returning from a trip over the ceiling.

John Bowman did not often go to church. This had been one of the mornings when he did not exactly know what to do with himself, and, not enjoying his own company well enough to stay at home without something interesting to read, had gone, just because he did not know what else to do. He had not listened to the sermon. Not he. He had thought of a thousand different schemes for employing that hour since he had been in church, and he wished with all his heart that he had stayed at home and carried some of them out. He resolved that it would be some time before he came again.

Katharine, wondering whether she had a work, and how she could begin to put on that yoke, glanced at her brother and in some way connected him with the sermon. She remembered her father's sentence at the dinner table some days before, "If you would devote a little more time to your brother, he might turn out more to your liking," and, sighing, wished she could do something in that direction. She watched him not a little during the closing hymn, and tried to think up some way of helping him. Nothing occurred to her except the evening service. She remembered having heard among the announcements of a young people's prayer meeting. She had a vague idea that it was by prayer meetings and churchgoing that people were made different; and perhaps John would get some good from attending. Anyway, it would keep him from going off with some of the boys who were doing him no good.

She decided, therefore, to try to get him to go that evening. To be sure, she had never been to the young people's meeting herself, and had an idea that it was a very dull affair; but the whole service that morning had been so in harmony with the little poem she was growing fond of, that she was seized with a longing to go herself, and see if she could get some help. Having made the resolve to try and do something for John, she felt very meritorious; but when the afternoon came, and the evening drew on, and she met John in the hall on his way his room, she found it was easier to resolve than to put into practice. Somehow, it was a very awkward thing for this sister to ask her brother to accompany her to prayer meeting. It was strange that all the cross, sharp words which she had ever spoken to him seemed to troop up and stand around now to listen. Perhaps it was their mocking, scornful presence that made Katharine's voice sound unnatural and her face take on a severe cast, as she finally mustered up courage and said, "John, I wish you would go down to the young people's meeting with me tonight."

John stopped short on the top stair, turned around, looked down on her, and drew a long whistle. "The dickens, you do!" said he in a surprised tone; then as he caught the severity of her face his own grew dark, his voice changed, and he said in quite a different tone, "How long since you've had to take up with your brother's company? You must be hard up if you can't scratch around and find someone else. Not much I won't! To prayer meeting? The idea! I didn't know you were fond of that sort of thing yourself." He gave a scornful laugh, and went to his room.

Of course it made Katharine very angry to have what she considered sisterly advances treated in this way, and she made up her mind never to try again. She went to her room in a fit of what she thought was righteous indignation, and treated her brother with a frigid dignity at the tea table. At the close of the meal, as he left the table, he said to her in an off-hand way, "I'm goin' down past the church, Kate; and if you want to go to that meeting, you can come along with me. There'll be plenty of folks for you to come home with. The Moffats always go, you know."

It was quite a condescension for John to say this; but Katharine was too much on her dignity to accept it. She spoke coldly, "Thank you; I can get there in the same way, then, if I care to go, without troubling you."

"All right!" John said, with a careless shrug of his shoulders, as he went out of the room.

Katharine did not go to the meeting that night. Instead, she shut herself into her room, and began thinking. She was very unhappy. At first the unhappiness vented itself in anger toward her brother, and a self-righteous feeling that she had done her duty; but this did not satisfy her. There seemed an emptiness about everything in which she tried to interest herself. She read the little poem over line by line, and tried to imagine herself saying it truly from her heart.

So peace and joy and love
Through all my being flow.

Why, peace was calm and deep and restful; and joy was uplifting; and love — why, love was the best, the sweetest, the greatest, the happiest thing in all the world! What would it be like to have them flow through all her being?

Do you know this blessed difference?
Do you long for this better way?

He will come to you as he came to me,
With the joy of an endless day.

Yes, she did long for this better way with
all her heart. Oh, would he come to her?
She bowed her head in her hands, and
burst into tears, wondering why she felt so
miserable. She had never felt so before.
She had never known these intense longings for something better, and could not
understand it now. She did not know that
at that very moment, away in a western
city, Cousin Hetty knelt in prayer, pouring
out her heart to God for her with an earnestness and faith that would not be de-
nied. Neither could she know that in one
of the rooms of an eastern college a young
man also knelt and prayed for her. Such
earnest, united prayers could not fail to
bring an answer. Katharine would have
been surprised to know that Frank Warner
was praying for her; for although she knew
he was one of the divinity students, and expected to become a minister, yet he had
never said or done anything to make her
think he took a special interest in her personal salvation or that of anyone else. But
since Frank had returned to college he had
met with some earnest souls who had put
new life into his own heart, and his con-

science began to reproach him for the long summer spent in idleness in the Lord's vineyard. As he grew nearer to the Master he began to have a great longing for his friends to come; and he thought of the bright girl who had been the life of their little company all summer, and wished that she, too, might find the Savior.

If Katharine had known all this, it might have hastened her decision. While she sat in her room, desolate and perplexed, her mind went back to the morning sermon, and a few sentences of it came clearly before her: "Christ says, 'Come unto me.' The first duty of a sinner is to *come*. One must not seek to appease an offended God by doing good works. Your works are not accepted by him until you have obeyed him and 'come.' How shall you come? Kneel down before him. Tell him you are wretched and sorrowful; that you need him to save you; that you wish to give up all sin, and belong to him." "How simple that is!" Katharine said to herself. "Why should I not do what he has told me to? If he wants me to come, why should I not? I will."

God's promise is sure. When Katharine arose from her knees she was surprised to discover what a new feeling of peace had come into her heart. She went to her window, and looked out upon the clear, starlit October sky. The bright lights shining there so steadily and kindly seemed to look down on her like the eye of God; and there came to her a sudden realization that now she could repeat the poem, and feel that she meant every word of it.

I *was tired yesterday, but not today.*
I could run and not be weary,
This blessed way;
For I have his strength to stay me,
With his might my feet are shod.
I can find my resting places
In the promises of God.

She turned from the window with a joy in her heart that had never been there before.

A WORK TO DO
While Katharine was getting breakfast Monday morning, old Andy came in with wood to fill the box behind the stove. He dusted his hands off, after laying the wood nicely in the box, and stood a moment with his rough fingers spread out before the fire. It was a chilly morning, and the warmth was grateful to those worn, hard-worked hands.

"Oh, an' wasn't that a sermon, Miss Katharine?" he said, as he moved his hands to let the warmth reach every part of them. "It jus' did my heart good. It jus' do seem that the preacher have the truth hid in his heart, an' he know how to tell it out too! An' that is a wonderful text, that is. I've been a-thinkin' about it greatly since you spoke of it last week. I have been a-thinkin' how we jus' ought to get right down on our knees an' thank the Lord every day that he be so kind an' willin' as to let us take his yoke upon us, an' that he will bear it with us. Instead o' that, we some of us go on every day, an' never so much as try to get the yoke to make the work easy. Why, Miss Katharine, I've many a time laid out to do a piece of work which I thought would benefit the Lord a great deal. I jus' went ahead and tried it, an' 'twouldn't work — o' course 'twouldn't. People, when they doos those things without consultin' the Lord to see if it's what he would have 'em do, has jus' got to make up their minds that 'twon't work. They ain't a-wearin' his yoke when they go on that line. Why, you see the verse goes on to say, 'And learn of me,' an' if they ain't a-learnin' of him they ain't got on his yoke, that's all. There's a heap of work a-lyin' round, ready cut out

42

an' basted, fur us to go at; an' if we prefer to go ahead an' cut out our own work, without even asking him fer his pattern and gettin' his advice, we kin decide it'll be a failure an' a botch; that's the whole story. That's what my mother used to tell the girls when they wanted to make their own dresses 'fore they was old enough an' wise enough; an' they tried it once or twice, an' they see 'twas jus' as she said. It don't pay to go to work 'thout learnin' of him." And the old man shook his head thoughtfully, and looked at the glowing coals.

"How can you learn of him, Andy?" asked Katharine. She was interested in this subject. It struck home. She thought of her own small attempt at work yesterday, and its failure, and wondered if here were not the secret of her difficulty.

"Learn o' him? Why, jus' go an' get acquainted with him. You want to read the Book about him, an' get so well acquainted with him as he was, that you know jus' what he'd do if he was in your place. Then you have to ask him to help, you know; an' he always do that. He allus carry the heavy end of the yoke hisself."

"But it would take a long time to find out all about him," said Katharine, "and

Mr. Richards said that people ought to go right to work as quick as they belong to him. One would have to read the Bible through to know all about him, and then they couldn't remember half they read."

"Oh, but, Miss Katharine, you do not need to wait. You go to our Father, an' he takes you, an' you ask him to put you to work, an' he says, 'I will, my child'; an' you ask him to take your wicked, sinful heart away, an' give you a good heart, an' he puts his Spirit in your heart, an' then you keep your eyes wide open, an' begin to learn about him, an' love him as fas' as you can, an' begin to love everybody else, an' you'll see plenty to do fer 'em. You grow so you find the work popping up at every turn. You may set it down as pretty sure that when you find a place you can't work in, or when you do something where you can't see a bit of work to do for him, then you better get out of it. It ain't the vineyard if there ain't any work in it for you, an' his children has no business anywhere outside of the vineyard fer a minit."

"But," said Katharine, half-laughing at the odd way in which he put it, "that can't be true, Andy, for that would cut a Christian off from ever playing any games, or having any good times."

44

"How so, Miss Katharine? I can't see 'twould work that way."

"Why, Andy, people can't do any good by playing games. There is no possible way in which they could do any work for the Lord that way."

"Better stop it, then, Miss Katharine. But I don't see it that way. There's that there pretty game you play out on my green lawn that I mowed so nice for you the other day, where you have a fishnet, strung up, and knock little white balls over it. I can't play it myself, but I like to see it, an' I feel every time when I see some of you young folks out there playin', an' a-seemin' to enjoy it all so much, that that's just what our Father wants us to do. I can think o' lots o' ways that there game might be made to come inside the vineyard. There ain't nothin' at all to prevent. I s'pose you could find a whole lot in this very town that would give their two eyes to get a chance at that there bat an' ball, an' be allowed to skip 'round on that pretty grass. Then you know we were told to go fishin' after other folks, an' bring 'em into the kingdom; an' it 'pears to me that there game would make jus' the best kind of bait. You young folks all seem to enjoy it so much, that it stands to reason other young

45

folks would too; an' if they could be given a chance, perhaps 'twould give you a hold on 'em, an' then the way o' the Lord would open wide enough, an' you would find the harvest in your corner o' the vineyard bigger than you could tend to all by yourself, an' you'd have to call in someone to help you. But I must be a-goin' now; I've got warm. You jus' try that game, Miss Katharine, an' see ef it don't make good bait. Good-mornin'."

Katharine was astonished over this part of the conversation. It had not occurred to her as possible that she could work by means of her pleasures. She had sorrowfully packed her rackets away in flannel only a day or two before, thinking that she should have no more tennis until the next summer. Hers was the only tennis court in the village, and she was the only one of the young people living there who played or understood the game at all. Now a new thought had come to her. Perhaps she might make her tennis help. She was very quiet at the breakfast table, thinking about it, but coming to no conclusion until she heard her brother say, "It's dreadfully boring nowadays. I wish there was a circus or a county fair or a baseball game to see, or something going on"; and he yawned and scowled, and looked out of the window in a hopelessly dreary way.

A thought came to Katharine. She waited a minute, considering it before she spoke, and then said, "John, suppose you come up this afternoon about half-past three, and play tennis with me."

It was said in a pleasant tone, and there was actually a smile on Katharine's face. John looked at her with amazement a moment, and then decided to take it all as a joke, and replied in a gruff tone, "I can't play tennis."

"Well, it's very easy to learn. I think I can teach you in a little while so that you can beat me. Boys always play better than girls after they get a start," said Katharine pleasantly.

"Do you mean it, really?" said John, looking pleased, and beginning to take an interest. "I always thought I'd like to play, but never could get a chance to get the hang of the thing when there wasn't anyone around watching. I didn't want to make a fool of myself, and none of 'em seemed to want me, anyway; so I kept out of the way."

It was strange what an effect this had upon Katharine. She felt ashamed and glad and sorry, all in one. To think that her

47

brother had wanted to join in her pleasure, and had been kept out partly by herself! Perhaps he might have been as good a player as anyone, and have learned many things from associations with the others. She was gleeful, too, to think that the "bait," as Andy had called it, had taken so well at the start. She resolved to do her best toward making her brother John love tennis as well as she did.

"But I haven't any racket," said John, a dismayed look coming over his face, as he suddenly thought of a new objection. But then he smiled.

"Oh, yes! there's one. Cousin Hetty left hers. She said it wasn't of any use to take it home, because she wouldn't be where she could play all the fall, and she expected to be back here early in the spring. She said I could use it whenever I wanted to."

Katharine went about her work after breakfast with a lighter heart than she had carried since her friends left. There was something very pleasant in anticipating a game of tennis, considering that she had not played for nearly a week, and that she had supposed that pleasure over for the summer. Then it was interesting to try to teach her brother. But beneath it all was a joy which she had scarcely begun to understand yet — the joy of doing work for Christ.

THE BAIT

The game of tennis was quite successful. John proved an apt scholar, and before long could hit the ball in a very commendable manner. Then, too, he gained a new respect for his sister when he found she could strike and place a ball so that he could not reach it. He made up his mind to become a good player, and be equal with her. So he put his will to it, and straightway won a game from her. They played on till called to tea, and then came in with bright eyes and glowing cheeks, laughing and talking together as their mother had not seen them do since they were little children. Katharine felt proud of John, and told with glee some comical remark of his to her father and mother at the supper table. Her father looked at her in a pleased way, and the mother dropped her anxious, worried expression. Altogether it was a very happy evening. John stayed at home, and Katharine spent some time in explaining to him the intricacies of a game with four players; and they decided that after he had had a little more practice they would try to get some of the other young people in town to purchase rackets and learn the game, so that they might have a full set. Really, John was growing almost as enthusiastic over it as Katharine. It was quite a new order of things for him to take such interest in home amusements, and it made his mother's troubled heart glad.

It became the rule now to play tennis every afternoon; and soon two other young people came to learn. The autumn was stretched out much beyond its usual length; and many days that were, strictly speaking, early winter, were warm enough to be delightful for tennis. There was no mistaking the fact that tennis had taken a firm hold on John Bowman, and was rapidly growing popular with several other young people in the village. Katharine, who had always been so reserved, and had kept much to herself when her summer friends were not with her, was becoming the center of attraction. She was rather astonished when she realized it herself, and remembered Andy's words, "I think that there game would make good bait." It was very evident that the bait was good, but she began to question whether she were using it in the right way. She had gone for several weeks to the young people's prayer meeting, and was becoming quite interested in it. She had even timidly ventured to recite a Bible verse once or twice; but she had never invited John since that first night in which he had repulsed her. Now she began to think about the matter again. He had not been to church since that Sunday when the sermon had so impressed her. She was much troubled about him. She was beginning to love him in a different, more interested way than she had ever loved him before. Indeed, she had been praying for him not a little lately, but in that timid, half-unbelieving way in which we sometimes pray for our friends, feeling that God has told us to do it. We wish them to be different, but we cannot see how it is possible that they can be changed. The wished-for alteration may come in the distant future, but in some mysterious, gradual way. Therefore, we feel no need for undue haste or earnestness.

Katharine had been thinking it over one morning, and had resolved that she would make another attempt to get John to the young people's meeting. She had just decided how she would introduce the subject, and was smiling over the way in which she thought her brother would reply, when she heard a ring at the doorbell, and went to answer it.

It was a young lady, a little older than Katharine, a member of the young people's society. She had come to see if Katharine would lead the next Sunday evening's meeting. She asked it in a quiet, matter-of-fact tone, as if she supposed, of course, it would be the most natural thing in the world for Katharine to say "Yes." But Katharine's heart came up and stood in her mouth in amazement and horror. She lead a meeting? No, indeed! She could not possibly do it! She was sorry they had thought of such a thing. She never could lead a meeting; she would break down.

Then the young woman looked at her kindly, and said, "Dear Miss Bowman, do you think it is right for a child of the heavenly Father to feel that way?"

"Right?" said Katharine in amazement.

"Yes, right. You have no physical inability. You are perfectly able to conduct the meeting. You help us in everything else. In all our socials and concerts and entertainments you are willing to take prominent parts. Why should you be unwilling, then, to lead the meeting? We all take our turn; why should you not do it too? You surely are not ashamed of your Savior?"

"No," said Katharine, with burning cheeks and eyes cast down; "but I'm sure I never could do that. I'm not good enough. Why, I've only just begun myself!"

"We do not any of us feel that we have much goodness, Miss Bowman; and I think you will find that even if you have just started out, this will be a help to you. It was to me. I felt stronger after I had done something like this. It is witnessing for him, you know. And really I think you exaggerate the duties of a leader. It is nothing so very difficult that you have to do. We usually open with singing once or twice, and then prayer and the reading of the Bible. The topic is selected on our cards, you know; and you can say a few words about the verses, or not, as you like. After that there are usually several short prayers. Why, the meeting will run itself; it only needs a head. But we want you very much to join in with us and help. Can't you do it for Christ's sake? He has done so much for us, you know; it seems a small thing for us to do for him."

But it required much more persuasion and argument before Katharine, with almost trembling lips, and eyes that were brimful of tears, murmured a low, "I will try."

Her heart trembled many times for the next few days over what she had promised to do, and she wished again and again that she could take back her promise. She spent many hours over her Bible, studying what she should say; but she did not carry out her plan for inviting her brother to attend the meeting. That was more than flesh and blood could stand, she thought, to lead a meeting, and have one's brother there besides.

Sunday morning came at last, and Katharine compromised with her conscience by asking John to go to church in the morning. He surely ought to do that; and it was not to be expected that it would be possible to get him to go twice in one day. John went to church, and really seemed to listen part of the time. Katharine spent the whole afternoon in her room with her Bible, and much of the time she was upon her knees asking God's Spirit to help her. She seemed to come nearer to her heavenly Father that afternoon than ever before, and to feel his hand upon her, and to hear his voice saying, "Be not afraid, neither be thou dismayed; for the Lord thy God is with thee whithersoever thou goest."

When she came downstairs, ready for meeting, there was a more peaceful expression on her face, and her heart felt a little more assured over the new duty which she was going out to perform.

But her brother John met her in the hall below. "Where are you going, Kathie?" he asked. "To that meeting? Guess I'll go with you, and see what it's like."

The Katharine of other days might have told him coldly that she did not wish his company, or preferred to go alone, or something of that sort; but she did not dare to do so now, after wishing so long that he would go.

They walked out the door and down the street in silence, the sister's heart throbbing painfully. How could she lead that meeting with her brother there? All her past inconsistencies and disagreeableness arose before her, and threatened to kill her with the awful weight of their immensity. She bowed her head in the darkness, and tried to press back the tears that were on the verge of rolling down her cheeks. At last she made a desperate effort at self-control, and said in rapid, trembling voice, "John, perhaps you won't like it if I don't tell you beforehand. *I'm* going to lead that meeting tonight."

It was out now; and she shuddered to think how hard it had been, and hoped

55

with her whole heart that John would say that he guessed he had better not go, that it might be embarrassing, or something of the sort. But no; he only drew a long whistle, and said, "The dickens, you are! Well, I'm glad I picked out tonight to sample it, then. I didn't know you ever did that sort of thing."

"I never did before, John. I don't know how I shall get on. But I am trying to please Christ now. I am almost afraid to have you go, because you will think I am not in earnest about it. I am afraid you will remember how many times I have been cross and ugly to you."

The tears had actually come now, and her voice was trembling.

"Why, Kathie," said her brother, almost tenderly, touched and embarrassed, and scarcely knowing what to say to this unusual outburst, "you're just splendid now! You don't get cross anymore — much. I wondered what it was about. But you can lead a meeting better than the whole lot of 'em put together, I'll bet. Don't you worry."

A NEW LAW
Her brother's words, spoken in that new tone of disguised tenderness, helped Katharine wonderfully. She went up to the

leader's seat by the little table with a feeling that she had one friend in the room at least. It was new to look to her brother for anything, and the last thing that was to be expected from him was encouragement. Could it be possible that he had learned this from her own helpful encouragement of him when he made a blunder in tennis? Katharine did not think of this as she took her seat and opened the hymnbook; she only knew that it was very pleasant to have her brother speak that way to her, and she felt a longing to have this meeting such as would help him to find Christ.

In the few words that she spoke when she bowed her head to open the meeting with prayer, she tried to forget that there was any one else present but herself and God, and she asked him to bless the meeting. The meeting did run itself, as the young committee-woman had told Katharine, and was a very earnest one. For her own part in it Katharine read the little poem which had grown so dear to her. She read it beautifully, putting her whole heart into it; and her brother, as he listened carefully to every word, noting with pride the distinct pronunciation and perfect expression, said to himself, "She means that. She feels every speck of it. She is different. I wonder what it all is, anyway." Then there came into his heart just the faintest little bit of a desire to know the wonderful difference himself.

When the meeting was over, John waited quietly for her at the door. He reached his hand for her Bible, and walked beside her without speaking for some time, but with an air of quiet respect, and an elder brotherly care of her which was quite new and pleasant. She could not speak first, her heart seemed so full. During the meeting a strange, earnest longing had come over her for him. She wanted so much to have him know the love of Christ.

"That was a first-class meeting, Katharine," he said at last, breaking the silence with an almost embarrassed tone. "None of them can go ahead of you on leading, *I* know. You can do most anything you try, anyway."

Then the longings of the sister's heart arose to her lips: "O John," she said, her voice trembling with earnestness, "I don't know how to lead meetings, nor do any of these things. They are all new work to me; but I mean to learn, and I do wish so much you would help me!"

It was John's turn to be surprised now.

He almost stopped short on the sidewalk with astonishment. "Me help!" he exclaimed. "What on earth could I do? I'm not worth much. You've told me so yourself hundreds of times."

"Oh, I know it, John!" she said in a pained voice, the tears coming quickly to her eyes, "and I'm *so* sorry. It wasn't true, and you could help me more than any other person."

"How in the world can I help you? What is it you want me to do?" asked John, quite tenderly and anxiously. He was not used to being asked by his sister for help, nor to seeing her in such a mood.

"Help me by trying to be a Christian with me. Won't you?" she asked eagerly. "We could work together, and help each other then; and I do so want you to belong to Jesus. Will you, John?" She put her hand lovingly into her brother's, and waited for his answer.

He closed his fingers about her hand with a warm, earnest pressure, and there was a manly expression on his face. He was very much touched. Perhaps his heart was all ready for the invitation, only no one had ever before given it. "What would I have to do?" he said at length, hesitatingly. Katharine had waited for his reply with her heart throbbing, and sending up eager, longing prayers to her Father in heaven to send his Spirit to speak to this dear brother.

"I am afraid I do not know very well how to tell you," she said, clasping his hand a little tighter in token of her great joy that his answer had not been "No." "I've only just begun myself, you know. The first thing is to give yourself to Jesus Christ. Tell him you want to be forgiven for all the wrong you have done, and you will be his forever, and try to please him always. Then after that pray every day for help, and read the Bible, and try harder all the time to please him. I'm only just finding out myself how to do it, and I want you to help, you know. You won't say no, will you? Oh, I need you so much!"

John hesitated, started to speak two or three times, then waited, and Katharine made several earnest pleas, always ending with her petition, "O John, won't you do it?"

At last, just as they reached their own gate, he said in a low voice, so low it was almost a whisper, "I guess so. I'll try."

"O John, I'm so glad!" she said joyfully; and she reached up to her tall young brother and kissed him. He bore the kiss with much embarrassment, and yet was pleased that she should give it. Katharine had never shown him much that she loved him, and he felt very tenderly toward her tonight. It was pleasant to have his sister care whether he became a Christian or not, pleasant to have her want his help. They went in the house together quietly then; and the father and mother noticed the expression on their faces with wonder as they entered the room.

After that the brother and sister began to get acquainted with one another as they had never done before. They had many talks together about this new subject which was beginning to interest them. John was very shy whenever Katharine spoke about it, and yet he seemed pleased. He entered into the agreement with her at first more from a desire to please her; but little by little he grew to understand how much the promise he had made meant. Katharine watched over him constantly, guarding him from temptations as often as she could. She became wonderfully entertaining, so much so, that John began to prefer to stay at home, instead of wandering off with "the fellows." Gradually their religious talks grew longer, until it came about that every Sunday afternoon, as a matter of course, John drew up a large armchair in the library bay window, and settled himself on the sofa opposite, motioning Katharine to take the chair. Then the two would read and talk together. They were trying to study the Bible in such a way as would give them practical help in their daily living, but did not always know the best way to do it.

Thus the autumn slipped into the winter almost without their knowledge, and they grew daily more attached to one another, and more bound together in all their duties and enjoyments. Helping each other, they helped themselves.

Christmas came, and with it many beautiful remembrances from the summer friends. Katharine opened them in surprise, and almost sighed as she opened one small, thin package, neatly wrapped in white paper, and addressed in a bold, clear hand. Then she gave her undivided attention to the package, and to the letter accompanying it. The opened paper disclosed a small white-clad book with gold letters. *The Greatest Thing in the World* was the title. On the flyleaf was written, "A Merry Christmas and Joyful New Year, from your friend, Frank Warner." Katharine's cheeks flushed and a pleased look came into her eyes as she turned to the letter. It read:

My dear Friend,

The accompanying little book has helped me very much, and I pass it on to you in the hope that you will enjoy it as much as I have. It is Professor Drummond's address on that wonderful love chapter, 1 Cor. 13. You will notice that he asks all who will to read that chapter every day for three months. I have begun to do so. Will you join me in it for the first three months of the new year? And may the greatest, the best thing in all the world be yours, is the wish of your friend,

Frank Warner

The next Sunday afternoon the new book was brought out and read; and not only the sister, but the brother, joined the young man in reading that marvelous chapter every day. It opened up to them new thoughts. Assisted by Professor Drummond's clear, helpful words, they studied Paul's analysis of "love," and tried to measure their own lives by it, and alter them so that they would fit the perfect pattern.

TOMORROW

It was a lovely spring day. The air was soft and caressing; the tender young leaves, which but the week before had first revealed their yellow-green edges, were dancing merrily, trying to shake the wrinkles out of their new spring dresses. The grass was made over new for the year, and was spangled with great bending daisies and saucy, nodding buttercups; and the clear blue sky looked down with just as pleased and surprised an air as it had used for all the other bright spring days of all the centuries gone before.

About the little village station the greenness and springiness crept, even up to its very door. Down the track a few yards the great black drinking hose which the engines used stood grinning, now and then sending a large, bright drop down with a gleeful splash, which bounded into little sprinkles over the board below. The bright steel rails gleamed in the sunshine, and hummed a cheerful prelude for the train that was approaching.

Katharine and her brother came with rapid steps down the street to the station. There was an eager, expectant look on Katharine's face that betokened some unusual pleasure. The house they had just left betokened it too. The windows were open, the summer curtains airing their freshness in the breeze. Little vases of spring blossoms stood around on tiny stands; and everything seemed in summer holiday attire. And the curtains, as they blew; the rooms, in their quiet unclutteredness; the flowers — all seemed to say joyfully, "Cousin Hetty and the rest are coming today, and we are ready and glad."

All but John. He had been dreading the summer. Katharine was beginning to be "so nice"; and now, of course, all their good times would be broken up. She would go off with the rest, and he would be left to himself. He did not blame her; but he sighed a little, and looked glum over the prospect. He had objected decidedly to accompanying Katharine to the station.

"They don't know me much, and won't want to see me; and I shall feel like a cat in a strange garret," he had said.

But Katharine had drawn her arm through his, and, looking up lovingly into his face, had answered, "I intend they shall know you 'much,' and if they care to see much of me, they would better want to see you too; for they will soon find out that I can't get along without my brother."

Of course John went after that, though

he did not in the least wish to; but he thought if Katharine wanted him so much he might as well gratify her.

The train proved to be seven minutes late; and as they stood on the platform waiting, Katharine looked off at the purple hills, which seemed to have planted themselves at the end of the track, and thought of that other day when she had looked gloomily forward at the winter, just passed. How bright it seemed to her now! What a difference there was in her life! It was no longer made up of much dull work, with only the little play spell of summer thrown in at long intervals, but was bright and happy all the way through. The coming of her summer friends she looked at in a different light now. It was indeed a delight to think of seeing and being with them once more; but it was, after all, but a pleasant incident, and not at all the one end and aim of existence, as heretofore. She looked at her brother proudly, comparing him with what he used to be, and wondering if the rest of the young people would see and appreciate him as she did herself. But the shriek of the whistle interrupted her meditations.

After that there was a merry bustle, a thumping of trunks, a babel of happy voices, and general confusion. John took the checks, and kept himself usefully in the background; but his sister brought him proudly forward as soon as possible. All the way home Katharine surprised the travelers by constantly appealing to John on questions connected with church work.

"I didn't know there was so much in John Bowman," said one of the girls in an undertone to her companion.

"I think he must have changed a good deal," was the murmured reply.

Notwithstanding, this same young woman was disappointed that afternoon when the girls, being eager for a first game of tennis, begged Katharine to bring her racket and help make up the set, and she replied, "I shall be busy for a little while this afternoon, but John will take my place."

There was nothing to be done but gracefully accept the situation and begin the game. She felt sure John Bowman could not play, and did not enjoy the prospect of being his partner. She changed her mind, however, before an hour had passed, and voted him a "splendid player, really quite scientific, besides being very pleasant company." Gradually they all came to accept him and enjoy him just as Katharine had intended they should.

But over his sister they were much puzzled. The Katharine of last summer was not wont to be occupied with anything that took her from their company, unless earnestly solicited by her mother to come and help her. This Katharine was busy from morning till night, and happy through it all. When she was with them, she was, as always, the life of the company; but she went from them to some duty with a complacent face, as though she really liked to go. Then she not only attended and enjoyed the prayer meetings of the church, but seemed to expect them to do so also.

When the little, leather-bound diary was brought out and read, the girls found the records very different from those they had expected. There were, indeed, many bright and original sentences, and there were whole pages of descriptions — beautiful, tender, witty, and unusual. There was a something left out, however, especially in the later entries, which had given the former Katharine's speeches much fascination, but could hardly be called quite charitable. Katharine was learning the old law of love, and putting it into practice. There were so many sympathetic, thoughtful touches in the small book, that they filled the place of the sharp sarcasms which were not present.

Cousin Hetty smiled to herself as she watched Katharine, filled almost with wonder to see how the soul in her had grown.

"She is indeed a child of the King," she wrote to her mother; "she shows it in every word and action, and John is not far behind her. Not that she is so very 'good,' as people say, or that she has attained to any perfection, but she seems to recognize Jesus Christ as the Leader of her life, the One first to be pleased always."

The young men noticed it too, when they came, and one of them felt that a prayer of his had been answered. Indeed, Frank Warner felt, as he watched Katharine day by day, that she had gone far beyond him in her Christian life.

"Miss Katharine, you seem different this summer from last," he said to her one evening as they walked down the moonlit village street, the last of the procession of young people who had gone out to enjoy the full moon. "Will you tell me how it is?"

"Am I different?" she asked, with a happy little laugh; then, more soberly, "I'm glad you think so. There ought to be a great difference, but there isn't as much as I wish."

"And what has made this difference? May I know about it?" he asked.

She was still for a moment, and then slowly, almost timidly, began to recite the little poem which had grown to seem a part of her life.

"I was poor yesterday, but not today;
For Jesus came this morning,
And took the poor away."

Through to the end she repeated it, her voice very sweet and low; and he listened, taking the words into his heart, to be kept for a sacred memory.

"That is the reason why there is a difference," she said, "if there is any. The restlessness and uneasiness are all gone from my heart now. I feel as if Jesus had forgiven me. Your little book has helped me too. I have read that chapter of Corinthians every day this year, and it grows more wonderful every time I read it."

The moonlight sifting through the leaves made a corridor of soft light for them to walk in. The hum of the crickets, the occasional lifting of some leaf by the night wind, and worried song of a mother bird singing a late lullaby to her babies — all seemed to lend a solemn quiet to the air about, and to help them to talk about this great subject, and open their hearts to one another as they had not done before. Gradually the voices of the others grew fainter, as the steps of these two grew slower, and they held sweet conversation about their heavenly Father. It seemed, indeed, as though he were near, listening; and when, in the quietness of her own room that night, Katharine thought over that walk and talk, the words of a familiar old poem came to her mind.

And the Lord, standing quietly by
In the shadows dim,
Smiling, perhaps, in the darkness,
To hear our sweet, sweet talk of him.

There came a day, at the close of the summer, when Katharine stood beside the front gate once more, thinking. The summer friends had all flitted again, and another winter was about to begin; but Katharine was not dreaming of her yesterday this time, nor even of her today, but was taking a little peep into a very bright tomorrow — a tomorrow in which she was to help Frank Warner be a good minister, and he was to help her be the minister's wife.

John came down the walk and stood beside her, resting his hand upon her shoulder. She looked up at his face, and saw in it a little of that sense of left-aloneness which had made her so miserable a year ago, and she roused from her sweet thoughts to cheer him up.

But John will never be troubled by the dreariness of a today; for his sister no longer lives in her yesterdays, and he has learned the secret of marking all the todays bright by looking forward to a joyful tomorrow.

An Excuse for Christ

It was Wednesday evening, and the minister's family had just returned from prayer meeting. The minister threw himself wearily into one of his low study chairs, and shaded his face with his hand. The bright moonlight streamed through the window by his side, and made a soft pathway over the carpet at his feet, but he did not notice it. Through the open door another pathway of light from the hall lamp almost met the moonlight. The minister's wife stood in this pathway, and threw a long shadow across the room. She was slowly pulling off her gloves, and casting uneasy glances at the dim outline of her husband. Lily, her young sister, who was there on a visit, stood in the hall by the hat rack, taking off her hat, and pushing up the fluffy hair on her forehead.

Presently Mr. Murray broke the silence. "We might as well give up the prayer meeting. The people won't come."

"Why, James!" exclaimed his astonished wife. "Give up the prayer meeting! You

73

surely don't mean that!"

"I do mean it. Just look at it, Mattie. Here it was a lovely night, the church was brightly lit, everything was favorable to a good attendance. And who was there? Old Deacon Eldred and his wife, who are hardly able to come out, and Mrs. Moker, who is too deaf to hear a word that's said, and Father Fisk, who always makes the same prayer, and the two Brunig sisters, and no one but yourself and Lily who could sing at all. It's a mere farce calling it a church prayer meeting. There are two hundred and fifty-seven members of this church, and there weren't but seven out to meeting. It would be a great deal better to invite them to our house than to have them rattling around in the four corners of that large room." Here the minister smiled a sad, faint smile, and leaned back again in his chair.

"It's a perfect shame!" said his wife, as she untied her bonnet strings.

"I'm sure I've tried to make the meetings interesting," came from behind the minister's hand; "but Deacon Eldred always goes to sleep — he's getting old, you know — and Father Fisk doesn't understand anything but the very simplest sentences. If only more would come!"

"Never mind," said Mrs. Murray. "We haven't been here very long, and you know they told you the people were not in the habit of attending the prayer meeting regularly. Perhaps they will do better after a while. Why, we haven't been here but eight weeks! You make the meetings so interesting that they can't help but come soon, I'm sure."

"My dear!" said Mr. Murray, in a tone bordering just the least bit on the impatient, "how can they know that the meetings are interesting when they don't come near them to find out? I can't understand how people who are under covenant vows to attend the regular services of the church can have so far forgotten their vows as to habitually stay away from prayer meeting."

Lily turned away from the glass with a last brush of the hair, and went to the doorway. "They ought to have such an article in their church creed as we have in the constitution of our young people's society of Christian Endeavor at home," said she.

"What is that?" asked Mrs. Murray in a rather abstracted tone.

"Why, they are required to send a written excuse when they are absent from the regular monthly consecration meeting, and it must be an excuse that they can conscientiously give to God. The excuses are read in the meetings, and it adds a great deal of interest, I assure you. The night before I left was our monthly consecration meeting. Several were obliged to be absent, and the excuses they sent were very helpful. I remember Fred Burton wrote, 'I am sorry not to be able to be with you this evening, but the Master's work calls me in another direction. Young Philips is very low, and I must stay with him tonight. May I ask that he have the prayers of the meeting?' And Lucy Reynolds wrote, 'Illness keeps me at home tonight, but my heart is with you.' Oh, we have such good times in our Christian Endeavor Society, Mattie!" and Lily launched into a full account of their doings at home, which continued till she bade them good night.

The minister heard no more. He had a new thought which must be turned over in his mind. He was his own cheerful self the next morning, and seemed to have forgotten all about his small prayer meeting.

The days slipped by pleasantly enough, and Sunday dawned. The congregation had just settled themselves into sermonful repose. The minister was reading the last notice, as they supposed — that same old one about the weekly prayer meeting which had grown so familiar that it seemed to go in one ear and out of the other. But Mr. Murray did not open the Bible and announce his text as they expected he would do. Instead, he stepped a little farther toward the front of the platform, and said, "Will all the members of the church who are unable for any reason to be present at the prayer meeting this week, please send an excuse in writing, on or before Wednesday evening, that it may be read at the meeting. It will be very pleasant to feel that we have the prayers and sympathy of the friends who are obliged to be absent. Any excuse which we can conscientiously give to the Lord Jesus Christ will answer the purpose, and will give those of the members who are present the feeling that your heart is with us, although your body cannot be there."

Only these few words, and he opened the Bible and announced the text they had waited for; but they did not hear it. They were a startled audience, or perhaps it would be better to say a company of startled individuals; for those who were in the habit of staying away from meeting of course did not know who else stayed away too, unless they were in their own family or their own immediate circle of friends, and so considered themselves, and not the whole congregation, addressed. Mr. Murray might have recited the Shorter Catechism, or a few pages of the dictionary or encyclopedia, that morning, so far as his sermon was heard by some of his audience.

Deacon Eldred, not being hit, went to sleep as usual. Poor old Father Fisk never understood the sermons. Mrs. Moker was deaf, and the Brunig sisters were not there. Mrs. Murray was too much occupied in imagining what people would think about Mr. Murray to give much time to the sermon, though it was one of his very best; and Miss Lily was very much occupied in studying the faces about her, and finding out what people did think.

Mrs. Hannibal Humphrey, under her new spring bonnet, was thinking something like this, "The perfect idea! Send an excuse to him! What business is it of his, I should like to know, what my excuse is for staying home from prayer meeting?" She kept herself strictly to that point; for it was rather uncomfortable to think back to last Wednesday night, and see herself leisurely reading an intensely interesting book. However, she was ready for this point if her conscience should bring it up. She might say that the book had to go back to the library the next day, and would require the evening to finish it, and she had no other time in which to read it. But her conscience did not bring it up. It knew it was of no use. Close by her side sat Mr. Hannibal Humphrey. He was not a member of the church. He did not consider himself included in the request that the new minister had made; but he thought it immensely amusing, and occupied the remainder of the hour in trying to frame an excuse for his wife. He often wrote responses to invitations for her, and on the way home he asked whether she would have it read.

My dear Pastor,

I am obliged to be absent from prayer meeting this evening, as we are invited to a small company at Mrs. Sullivan's, to meet their friend Miss Rochester, who is to leave town the next day. I am sorry I am unable to meet with you; but you see how it is.

Very truly,

Mrs. Hannibal Humphrey

Or did she intend, after all, to send regrets to Mrs. Sullivan's, and have the card party she had spoken of that morning? In that case it should read:

Dear Mr. Murray,

I am sorry to be absent from the meeting Wednesday evening; but we have arranged to have a few friends to spend the evening, and have a quiet game of cards. I should be glad to have you and Mrs. Murray step in after meeting.

Very truly,
Mrs. Hannibal Humphrey

"Perhaps, though," he said, as he handed her gravely the slip from his hymnbook, on which he had written the sample notes during the closing prayer, "it would be as well to leave off that closing sentence, as the thing is to be read in the meeting, and some of the rest might feel hurt unless they were invited too." But for some reason Mrs. Humphrey seemed not to wish to talk upon the subject, and told her husband that she thought he was very irreverent, whereat he laughed long and loud, disturbing Mrs. Humphrey's feelings still more.

Miss Effie Summers was a church member, but she could hardly remember when she had been to prayer meeting. Her aimless little mind began to search about for a reason why she had never been, and she had to admit to herself that it was because

80

she had never thought of it. She almost smiled in church at the idea of herself at prayer meeting. It had never occurred to her as a place where she would care to go. She looked down at her gloves, and admired their fit, and wondered if, after all, the ones with the darker stitching on the backs would have been a better match to her suit, and remembered that it was last Wednesday afternoon that she had bought them; and that she had lounged in a big chair all the evening, eating cream-dates and talking nothings with her young cousin who chanced to come in, and never once thought there was a prayer meeting. She made her silly little heart keep still by telling it that not thinking of a thing was a good excuse for not doing it, although there was a slight question somewhere which interfered with the satisfaction she felt in the fit of her gloves, and made her wonder whether she would like to stand up before the great God and offer that excuse.

Mr. Worcester, just at her left, a tall, stern man of business, dismissed the prayer meeting subject with these words: "I really haven't time for prayer meeting. My hands are too full of business cares. I go to church on Sunday, and I'm sure I give a great deal to support the gospel, and that is all that can be expected of such a busy man as I am"; and his mind went off to a certain knotty point that he had not been quite able to decide the day before.

Will Kenton glanced uneasily over at Effie Summers. He was a member of the church too; but he had arranged it in his sleek little head that very morning that he would call upon Miss Effie Wednesday evening, and secure her company to the concert before that fellow from Boston got ahead of him. Miss Effie wouldn't be likely to go to prayer meeting. To be sure, he didn't go often enough himself to know who went, but he knew her well enough to hazard a guess. Effie looked very pretty, and there was no other evening on which to call; for Monday evening was his club, and Tuesday was the whist party. Just then the new glove went up to see if the new hat was straight, and the hand looked so very pretty that it carried the day. Then he told himself he really must go this time, and he would try and arrange for the prayer meeting another week.

Tired little Mrs. Carroll heard the request with dismay. Here was something else that ought to have been done. She was so overcrowded with cares that she didn't know which way to turn now. She thought back to last Wednesday night. She had just finished the twenty-seventh tuck in Lucy's white organdy that afternoon, and was so tired she could hardly finish the tea dishes. She sat back easier then. It surely wasn't her duty to go to prayer meeting when she was so tired it would have made her sick; yet she wondered dimly in her weary brain if, after all, that tuck hadn't been to blame, and whether she had any right to get so tired before the meeting. Would she like to present a tuck as her excuse to the Lord for not having attended his meeting? Her heart was not at rest. There was another sister who remembered herself as having been too tired to go last Wednesday; and she wondered if it would be necessary, in order to be strictly true, to say that she had been making pound cake all afternoon.

Mr. Mosley remembered with grim satisfaction that he had had the neuralgia last Wednesday, and had not thought it prudent to go out in the evening air; but he forgot that half an hour after the bell had ceased ringing he had gone to the door with Mr. Patterson, who had called on business, and there he had stood for a full fifteen minutes in a chill east wind, without so much as an overcoat or hat to protect him.

There were many who did not think at all, and who forgot the minister's request almost as soon as it was made, who had no idea of going to prayer meeting, and who did not know as they ever would have. There was one young lady who declared on the way home that she never went to prayer meetings, because she did not enjoy them. She thought they were poky places, and made one feel awfully doleful. Her brother told her he thought that was an excellent reason — and would she like to have him write the excuse for her? He would get it up in fine style; and he thought it would be better than most of the excuses other folks would write, because it was true, and no made-up reason. "All the same, Lou," said he, "I can't say I would like to give it to the One who is to test your excuses." Then he whistled. He had never said anything so solemn as that in his whole life before, and he did not exactly know his own voice. And the sister said, "Oh, nonsense!" but she did some thinking on the way home.

There was much talk at the various dinner tables of that congregation that day. Some thought the new pastor had taken a good deal upon him, and that he had no right to make such a request. "I suppose I might 'a' let the horses rest 'a' Wednesday afternoon, and not plowed the medder lot till Thursday," said Farmer Stevens, as he took a bite of pork, and shoveled some beans into his mouth with his knife. "We ain't been to prayer meeting in a good while. I reckon we'd better try to go this week." Meek little Mrs. Stevens' face brightened, and she said she'd be real glad to go. She had missed the prayer meeting, but she had never said so, and they lived so far out she hadn't thought it possible for them to go.

The Haines household discussed the matter at the dinner table. Little Nannie sat and listened, and, after turning it over in her mind for a time, bluntly asked of her elder sister, "Kit, why didn't you go to prayer meeting last Wednesday night? Oh, I remember! Your bonnet had just come home, and you didn't like it, and tore it all to pieces to fix it over. Wouldn't it 'a' been funny if you had written to Mr. Murray, 'Please excuse me from going to the meeting, 'cause my bonnet don't look right, and I have to trim it over'?" Amid the general laughter that followed, Miss Kittie told her sister she was a saucy little thing, and went to her room to quiet her upset nerves. There were some few who spent the

Sunday afternoon hours in serious thought and in making many resolves which meant much for the future of that church prayer meeting.

Sunday passed, and Monday and Tuesday. Wednesday came; the sun went down behind some lovely clouds, and the moon sailed out, with here and there some attendant blinking stars, and the bell for evening worship pealed out. The minister took his Bible under his arm, waited a moment for his wife and Lily to pass out, then locked the door; and together they went down the street. Mrs. Murray felt decidedly nervous. Miss Lily, also, was a little excited, for from the other direction, she could see the two Burnside girls with their brother, and she couldn't help wondering whether it could be possible that they were coming to the meeting. But Mr. Murray walked silently along, not joining in the little hum of talk that his wife and her sister kept up. He was thinking of what he was to say to his people, and he felt no nervousness about the meeting; for he had spent much time in prayer that afternoon, and he knew that the meeting was in the hands of his heavenly Father, to prosper as he would.

Early as they were, when they opened

the door they saw the long rows of usually empty seats nearly filled, and more people were coming down the street. Lily noticed in surprise that the Burnsides were really coming up the steps. Various forces had combined to bring these people there.

Miss Effie Summers was there because she had not anything to do, and it was a lovely night, and she had thought of it, and there really was not any reason why she should not go, just for once, and she supposed she ought to go sometimes, anyway. Besides, it troubled her to think that she would need to present her excuse to the Lord. So she was there, and, upon being whispered with for a few minutes, reluctantly consented to preside at the organ. Will Kenton came in a little late, and somewhat flurried, having been to call upon Miss Effie; but upon being told that she had gone to meeting, he, in much amazement, had bowed himself out, and made his way to the church.

Mrs. Hannibal Humphrey was not there; but she had an excuse. She was neither at Mrs. Sullivan's tea party, nor entertaining company herself. Instead, she had retired to a dark room with a sick-headache. Her unfeeling husband told her she had good taste, for he thought on the whole it would sound much better than either of the excuses he had written. However, she sent no excuse. Mr. Humphrey was there himself. It came about in this way. He had lounged around in the room, and read all the papers through, and it seemed very dull. Supper eaten all alone was a gloomy affair, and Mrs. Humphrey did not seem inclined to talk when he went up to see her. Then the church bell rang; and the thought came, why should he not go to meeting? He believed he would go, just to see if there would be any excuses, and what they would be, and who would be there. He might be able to get some fun out of it; it certainly was dull enough at home. So he went.

Mr. Worcester was there because all the plans he had laid out for that evening came to naught. The man with whom he had made an appointment sent word he could not come; the book he had intended reviewing he had forgotten, and left in his downtown office; and the letters he had thought to answer did not come at all, the mail-train being delayed by an accident. The bell rang, and Mr. Worcester in despair took himself to the Lord's house.

Mr. Mosley did not have the neuralgia; and, being a prominent member of the church, he thought it would not do to utterly ignore the new pastor's request, and so he went. Mrs. Carroll dragged her weary self to the church because her conscience troubled her for having allowed Lucy to coax her into buying her a dark-blue surah, and she hoped to find some peace of mind in going as a sort of penance. Not that she put it that way. She would have been shocked if you had suggested such a thing, and she kept it strictly a secret from her better self. The pound cake woman even refrained from making an elaborate dish for tea that night so that she might come to the meeting.

There were of course the few faithful ones who always came to prayer meeting when they could, because they loved it, and because the Lord had promised to meet his children there and bless them; but they were not so very many.

And so, for various reasons, these people had taken their bodies up to the house of the Lord to spend a little time in communion with him; and the Lord looked and saw the hearts all taken up with the cares of this world, and longed to bless them, but saw that some minds were far from his church and his worship.

At the door, Father Fisk, who acted as

sexton, handed Mr. Murray two notes. One was crumpled, misspelled, and nearly illegible.

Dear Mr. Murray,
I am laid up with the rumatiz, and can't com to the meetin', but my heart is with you. May the Lord be there. Your humble servant,

Susan Moker

The other was from Deacon Eldred, written in a trembling hand.

Dear Pastor,
My precious wife who has traveled beside me for so many years has passed on before. I trust I may have the prayers of God's people tonight in my deep sorrow.

Oh, that meeting! It was a revelation to some of those who didn't usually attend.

"I never dreamed a prayer meeting could be so interesting!" said Miss Effie merrily, as she laid her hand on young Will Kenton's arm, on the way down the church steps after meeting. She had been prevailed upon to play the organ, and she had done it well. Will Kenton's rich tenor had swelled out with Mr. Hannibal Humphrey's bass, and carried other voices in such a tide of song as astonished the old church walls.

The minister's few words seemed to stir his audience as it had not been stirred in many a long year. A few repeated verses. One lady called for a favorite hymn. Mr. Worcester was moved to pray for Deacon Eldred in his great sorrow, and others followed.

They went out from that hour of prayer feeling as if they had received a blessing, and wanted to come again. Some wondered why they had never gone before.

Lily lingered in the parlor with her sister to talk over the meeting, and exult over the appearance of this one and that.

But the minister, alone in the moonlit study, knelt and thanked God.

John Chamberlain's Easter Coat

It was Monday morning, and the world had put on its workaday clothes again, and started the busy song of the week. Even the lazy clouds, which but the day before had been still and dreamy in their Sunday quiet, seemed to be scurrying across the sky with a purpose. The whiz and whir of machinery from the tannery and sawmill across the river could be heard distinctly. Everything seemed to be bustling about to get ready for spring to come. The withered grass, amid patches of dirty, discouraged looking snow that seemed about ready to take its departure, spruced up a little, and actually tried to send forth a faint green tinge in response to the warm sunlight.

A young man, a salesman perhaps, walked briskly down the street of the little village toward the two stores, with a large valise in his hand. He had a business air, even to the slightest detail of his dress. His

92

nicely fitting clothes reminded one of the bustling city.

But despite all the atmosphere of hurry that hung over the place, John Chamberlain still stood at his front gate.

He was watching the young man, presumably a salesman, as he hastened down the street. It was not so much the man, either, that his eyes were fixed upon, as it was his clothes. Any one could tell by a glance at those clothes that they were made by a city tailor, and they gave their wearer an air of grace and importance which John Chamberlain's clothes had never afforded. He knew the lines of that coat on the young man almost as well as his own; for he had studied their shape with careful eye during the whole of the sermon yesterday morning, envying the turn of the collar, and even the two jaunty buttons set behind. He looked down again at his own coat as the other disappeared within a store at the end of the street. What was it but an ungainly covering which always made him feel that his hands were encumbrances which were to be got along with the best way he could; that his joints were made of wood, and would not move at his bidding; and that his whole figure was utterly out of proportion in every direction?

He wished he could have a coat made by a real city tailor himself. He had never had one. Money was scarce. He despised these cheap, ready-made affairs he had worn since he had grown too old for his mother to make his clothes. He took out his knife, and cut spiteful little chips out of the fence post. Why should that fellow — meaning, of course, the salesman — wear such coats with that insolent, easy way, and he, John Chamberlain, have to wear these nasty store-made things that he despised? He had been given a good education, if he was poor, and the salesman did not look as if he had any brains worth mentioning. Yet Jessie had cast actual glances of admiration in his direction after church, and asked who he was. Of course the admiration was for the coat. Jessie was such a stylish, trim little thing! Here his face grew tender as the vision of the slender, dainty, bright-faced girl came before him — Jessie, who always seemed to be able to make a pretty costume out of almost nothing. Her clothes, nevertheless, made her look utterly unlike any of the other girls of the village, and set her well above them so far as style, though the others tried hard to eclipse her. His heart rebelled against a fact that kept him from having a coat that would merit admiration from Jessie. He felt sure he would be able to walk up the church aisle with as much nonchalance as the young stranger if he could wear the stranger's clothes, and not let his hands and feet get in the way.

There was much nicking of the fence post done that morning, for John Chamberlain was deciding an important question; but it was settled at last, and he started for his work. He walked down the street briskly, too, now. He had decided to have a new coat; and, once decided, it was almost as good as having it on his back that minute. Why, there was the entire variety of coats to choose from — Prince Alberts, sack-coats, business coats, and the whole world of coats! An evening suit even hovered dimly on the horizon of his mind, without any shadow of an idea of coming nearer to him, however; but it was pleasant to him to think of it as a possibility. He walked down that street in all the glory of the best-fitting clothes that the finest city tailor could make. His arms swung easily at his sides, and he was for once utterly unconscious of the red, bony appendages which he used for hands, and which had hitherto troubled him so much. Imagination can do a great deal. It even went so far as to make him raise his arm, covered at that moment with the prospective Prince Albert sleeve, which was to be bound with braid, and finished with two small, neat buttons, and touch his hat with as much grace of movement as a city salesman could possibly use, to Jessie as he passed her house; and she thought as she blushingly returned the salute, "What a fine figure John has! Strange I never noticed before how handsome he is growing!"

If he was going to have the coat, he might as well have it at once, he thought. In two weeks it would be the Easter vacation. Jessie's two brothers would be at home then for a few days, and she had said she wanted to have a little gathering for them. It would be very nice to have something new for that time. Indeed, now he thought of it, it was absolutely necessary that he have it for church on Easter Sunday. Why, it would be very embarrassing to have to attend church under the eyes of those college brothers with his old, ill-shaped coat! It certainly would not do. He would go down to the city the very next day and have his measurements taken, that the new one might be ready in time. This much settled, he went to his work with a light heart, and whistling a joyous tune. All day long as he went about his duties he saw himself as he would appear in the new garment. He felt the pleasure with which he would enter the church. It would be an unusual time, anyway. The church would be trimmed, and all the ladies would have their spring bonnets. John had a dim idea that a new bonnet was in some way connected with Easter time; and if bonnets, why not coats? Of course he must look his best. He would feel that he fitted in with the flowers and the extra music and all the gala attire, if he had his new coat.

But about the resurrection of Jesus Christ, that most marvelous of all the proofs that God has given us of his love and mercy, that wonderful story which makes us sure that we shall never die, John thought not one whit that day. Easter to him was a time of wearing new clothes; a time of the return of college brothers; a time of enjoyment that held all sorts of delightful possibilities for him. Not that he was not a Christian, this young man whose heart at that present moment seemed to be given over to dress. Why, he was to lead the young people's prayer meeting on that eventful Easter Sunday night; but he had forgotten about that entirely. When it did again enter his consciousness, it looked to him like a tremendous cross — especially under the existing circumstances of possibly sarcastic college brothers — which must be taken up and carried in the easiest way. Nevertheless, it would be easier if carried on the shoulders of a new coat. He could even think of himself quite composedly, as standing up before the desk in his new coat announcing a hymn.

On the whole, that meeting had a pleasant side to it; for after the cross had been borne and the meeting was over, he might persuade Jessie to let him walk home with her; and perhaps, if the evening was pleasant, and the moonlight bright, she would not mind walking on up the hill a little way. And then, *perhaps* — it *might* be — that he would feel the time had come to say something to Jessie which he had long wanted to say. It would all depend upon the effect of the new coat.

So the young fellow worked and whistled away, and thought his pleasant thoughts; and the night at last came when he could dream them all over again; and then the morning, with an early breakfast, and a rush for the fast express that would take him to the city in an hour and a half.

Then began a day for John. He had not imagined it would be so hard a task to do his shopping. He went from tailor to tailor, seeking exactly the coat of his ideal; but it proved hard to find, at least at the price he could afford to pay, for this young fellow had extravagant tastes, although he did not know it. They showed him one after another, and tried to make him think he would have a ready-made one; but he was firm. A coat made to order he would have, and no other; and at last, after weary searchings, he found the right piece of cloth, corresponding both to the size of his purse and his taste. It was with pride that he doffed his old coat that his measurements might be taken; and he drew his fine proportions up to their full height, and looked down upon himself as the tape measure went grimly around his chest. Soon he would have a coat that he could be proud of; and this tape measure was its harbinger, and, therefore, a badge of honor. Of course he did not really think all this, or at least did not realize that he was so doing, for John was a young man of too good sense to have said all this to himself; but there was the pleasant sensation of it in his soul which made him lean back in his seat in the homeward-bound evening train, and actually enjoy his ride home, weary though he was with his shopping.

With thoughts of himself in his new attire, John's days dragged slowly by until it should be done; and as the important Sunday drew near, he began to be anxious lest it would not be done in time. But the coat arrived from the tailor's, and Jessie's brothers from their college, on the same train on Saturday evening. John met them both at the station, a little chagrined, it is true, that he had to wear his old coat; but it was dark, and he kept well in the shadow. Besides, he felt a sort of gentle, stylish influence from the bundle under his arm, even through its several heavy wrappings. With the knowledge of what was inside that brown paper he could walk easily beside even college-bred young men.

They beguiled him into a scheme for the evening, the brothers and Jessie; and he came home rather late, the precious package still unwrapped, only to remember as he entered his room that he was the leader of the meeting for the following evening, and that he had not prepared for it in the slightest degree. He took down his Bible, and tried to make some little preparation then; but his eyes were heavy, and he soon gave it up. He had to have one look at his coat before his head touched the pillow. He untied the strings, and drew it from the paper; but just as he held it at arm's length, and shook out the folds, his kerosene lamp, which his landlady did not believe in filling very often, flickered and sputtered, and its gasping flame sank lower and lower. He turned it up impatiently, and tried to look again closely at the coat; but the flickering flame winked lugubriously, and gave warning that it would last but a moment more, and he had better hasten to his bed or he would be left in utter darkness to make his final preparations. He laid the coat carefully on his chair, and made all haste to obey, feeling it a little hard that he should be thus prevented from a scrutinizing view of this long-awaited garment. But he smiled as he turned out the light of the wicked, smoking lamp, and said to himself, "Never mind. It will be there in the morning. I can wait, and I'll enjoy it all the better then."

Then he went to sleep to dream of the pleasant evening he had passed, and of the morrow that might be so full of joy for him.

It was late when he awoke the next morning. The first early church bell was actually ringing. He sprang up, and dressed hastily, not caring to put on the new apparel until after he had been down to breakfast. Back in his room, he hastened at last to the coat. There it lay in all the glory of its newness and its supposed city fit. Its color was so very black and its buttons so very precise and trim, that he felt like apologizing for the blacking on his boots, brushed to a high polish though it was.

On went the coat; for there really was not much time left for admiration, if one was to get to the church before the whole congregation was seated. He buttoned the last button proudly, and stepped to the glass to survey himself.

Oh, horror of horrors! What was this? A cold chill began to creep upward, and a heavy feeling replaced his happiness. Could it be that it did not fit? What! A city coat not fit! A coat cut by a city tailor *not fit!* Why, no one ever heard of such a thing! There must be some mistake. He must have put it on wrong in some way. He gave it a decided yank upward, and then smoothed it over his shoulders with both hands, as a lady does with an ill-fitting dress, and then squared about again in defiance to the glass. But no; the collar sagged down in the back with the same dogged air as before. With despair he seized hold of the shoulders of the innocent thing, and gave it such a jerk toward his ears as could not fail to bring about a decided change in the set of the article. But the more fiercely he pulled and smoothed and raised his shoulders and ducked his head forward in his attempts, the more determined that collar grew to lop out and away from the shining linen it was meant to cover. The linen collar creaked and squeaked, the shirt bosom groaned, the necktie writhed itself till the bow was under one ear; but all to no purpose.

Disappointment was no name for the feeling in John's heart. He had not realized how thoroughly he had come to depend upon this new coat, nor how much his heart had been set upon it. If he had been a girl he would have cried; but being a man he did not understand himself, and his face grew red, and he tore around his room and glared at his crooked cracked looking-glass. To add to his confusion, the second bell for church began to ring, and soon he knew it would toll. He tried to calm himself, for certainly this coat must be worn to church if he went at all. It would not do to wear the old one after all the abuse he had heaped upon it during the week. He tried another collar not quite so high, and then one higher, a darker necktie too; but all seemed to make no difference. He brushed his hair over again savagely two or three times; but still his head continued to look as if it were going on ahead of him, with that coat collar like a rudder steering him. At last the bell was almost done tolling; he seized his hat and rushed down the street to the church, arriving there out of breath just as the choir began the opening anthem.

John Chamberlain thought as he entered the church and searched about for a seat — and none was to be found — that the eyes of the whole congregation were upon him and his coat collar. If he had seen the tailor who made it, I am not sure but he would have strangled him then and there. He remembered with mortification the delight with which he had contemplated himself in his mind's eye in this very coat; and now the reality was causing him more embarrassment than he had known in all the time he had owned his old one. Why, he had been well pleased with that when it was new. He had not expected anything better of it than to cover him and to look clean and new. He realized with a sense of pain that this one best coat of his which was to him so much, had been just a common, everyday affair to the tailor who made hundreds of them for common use by the city people. His painful thoughts were interrupted by hearing the announcement of the young people's meeting that evening; and he experienced that sudden, awful feeling that he was rushing on to a moment for which he was not prepared and for which he seemed to have lost all power to prepare.

But there did come a calm in this whirl of thoughts. It was during the singing, "I know that my Redeemer lives." The triumphant melody floated over the church, and John Chamberlain could but listen; for it was as if angels had charge of that music, and were wafting it to hearts, and not alone to ears. He did not understand why the thought that his Redeemer had risen thrilled him just then as it never had done before. Perhaps it was because the dear Lord was present there, ready to come to each troubled or doubting heart, even to John Chamberlain, sitting there in his new, disappointing coat, in the back seat, with his head bowed.

Surely he did come and bless that heart, for John felt a peace which he had not known before. It did not come from the sermon, for that was not so very wonderful, though John thought it was; but it must have been from the Master himself, for it stayed with him. John could not have told much of the sermon when it was over. Indeed, he felt very uncertain about the text. He only knew that he had been with the disciples as they took the body of Jesus from the cross and prepared it for the burial. He fancied he himself had helped to pour out the precious spices; he felt the sorrow in his heart, all the while, that the disciples must have felt when they thought they were doing the last bit of service for their Master; and then he seemed to have stood afar off and watched the stone as it was rolled to the opening in the tomb and a great seal set upon it. It was all very vivid to him. He was certain he knew how the disciples felt when the angel spoke to them; for the angel seemed to have spoken to him, and said, "Fear not, for he is risen." And after that he seemed to have talked with the Master himself.

The prayer which followed the sermon seemed to John to be conversation with a risen, present Savior, and not a talk addressed to a God afar off, as prayer usually seemed to him. He had forgotten his coat utterly. He was uplifted.

Jessie noticed him as he sat listening

with earnest, attentive gaze to the speaker. John was a handsome man, she thought, as she turned back to listen herself, and see what it was in which he appeared to be so much interested. She had not seen the ill fit of the coat collar, and was not sufficiently versed in coats to know that it was wrong if she had. John looked nice in her eyes, and she was glad.

Instead of going to walk as was John's custom on Sunday afternoons, and dropping in at Jessie's house perhaps, he stayed in his room. He felt that he had much to think about, and must be by himself. There was the meeting. It could not be passed by easily. After the impression the morning sermon made upon his heart, he did not dare to stand up there and lead the meeting in a perfunctory manner as he ordinarily did when it came his turn, without saying one word upon the subject himself, nor even leading in prayer, but rather calling upon someone else to do it for him, and shirking every possible duty that he could. For a little while that afternoon he felt that he must go to someone and say that he could not lead the meeting, he felt so unworthy; but the same Spirit that had been with him in the morning led him to a different frame of mind, until he was willing to kneel down and say, "Here, Lord, am I, unworthy though I am. Make me useful as thou wilt."

The new coat hung carelessly over a chair, forgotten while the owner studied his Bible. When John Chamberlain once more donned his proud apparel, there was indeed a slight feeling of regret and disappointed hopes connected with it; but it seemed of very little consequence now, in the light of the last few hours. One glance he gave at himself in the glass just before he left the room; and really the collar was not quite so bad after all, but lay almost meekly about his neck. He went down the street clothed not in fine raiment, as he had hoped to be, but in the quiet garment of humility. One thought was in his mind now, not of earthly apparel, but of spiritual; an old thought, which Paul expressed in these words: "For in this we groan, earnestly desiring to be clothed upon with our house which is from heaven . . . that mortality might be swallowed up of life."

"Now is Christ risen from the dead, and become the first fruits of them that slept." He could almost hear the words of the morning song echoing yet in his heart; and it brought new meaning to him now as he realized that he, too, would one day arise to be with Christ forever. Over and over in his mind ran the words, as he took that walk in the starlight while the bells chimed their joyful resurrection carols, "So when this corruptible shall have put on incorruption, and this mortal shall have put on immortality, then shall be brought to pass the saying that is written, Death is swallowed up in victory."

John and Jessie took that walk together after the service, just as he had thought they might. She had meant to stop at her own gate, of course. When they had reached it, John had been talking so earnestly about the meeting, and there had been such a longing in her own heart not to have the talk end, that she had yielded when he held her arm a little more firmly and said, "Just let us walk a little farther, Jessie; I'm not half through talking yet."

On they walked, not heeding how far after that; out where the road melted into still green fields, with mossy, sleepy-looking fences on either side; out where the soft gray clouds sweep overhead and do not look, and even the little trees by the roadside are asleep and cannot hear.

They had many things to talk about, for the meeting had been a very helpful one, and this was a resurrection day to these two hearts in more ways than one. Jessie felt how cold-hearted a Christian she had been for a long time, and she told John she meant to be different now; that he had helped her to some new thoughts which she would never forget, and that Christ was more to her than he had ever been before; and John felt his heart throb with joy and gratitude that, though he was unworthy, he had been used by the Master so soon.

Yes, and he did speak those words he had thought so long to speak, all unfitting as his coat collar was. I am not sure, though, that he would have dared to do so even in the glories of the salesman's stylish suit, if a cloud had not covered the moon often that night, and if his heart had not been so warm and happy about other things, that such small, insignificant objects as coats vanished into oblivion.

In due course of time, when the pain of the disappointment had disappeared, John told Jessie all about it, and she laughed with him, and cried about it too; for her true woman's heart saw between his comical sentences the keen disappointment he must have felt over the failure of his first "dress-up" coat to be all he had planned it should be. But when the laugh was over, and they were quietly and soberly talking about it, she said, "John, I'm glad it didn't fit, after all; for then you might have been complacent, and never come to have that wonderful feeling about the resurrection of Jesus Christ which filled you so full that it reached even to me. Dress is one of the things that leads people away from Christ. It must be one of the greatest things he meant when he said, 'Come out from among them, and be ye separate.' It always did seem dreadful to me to talk about Easter bonnets, as if they had any connection with the resurrection of Jesus Christ. Easter coats are not any worse than Easter bonnets, John; but I am glad it didn't fit."

A Voice Unheard

The sun was just bidding good night to a little summer resort, brushing its lake with many colors, lighting up the windows of its cottages, touching with glory its tallest treetops, and making that particular spot feel as if there were no other spot on earth quite so beautiful or so beloved by the sun. The lake had a peculiar look, as if it had been sweeping itself into small eddies just as the sun went down, and had caught itself in the act, and stood motionless to watch the light of his dying. One small sailboat, with its still white sail, lay upon the surface, and drifted so softly you would have thought it was becalmed. A little steamer going on its necessary evening journey seemed to ply its wheels more quietly, and to hush its noisy breathing, as if the place and the sight might be desecrated thereby. Two or three cranes whirled low and slow above the calm water, as though performing some solemn priestly office. It was plain that the sun had caught and held the attention of the earth and its creatures; for even the little birds hushed their chirpings, as with invisible hand the wonderful colors of the sky were changed, now from a delicate yellow — the light that would come from the sun shining through a bit of amber — into a suggestion of emeralds seen through a flood of glory light, then a flash of a rosy-colored banner above, to blend with the soft gray clouds into the deeper purple, and to grow into scarlet and dark crimson as the sun sank lower.

Only a few human witnesses were there that night, for it was late in the season. In fact, the season was already over, and there was but a handful of people remaining of all the throng who had visited that popular resort during the summer. The place seemed desolate now — so many cottages closed. It made the few lingerers long to seek the sunset every night as something which would be just as grand for its few observers as it had been all summer long for the crowds that had sought the summer-house on the summit of the hill by the lake. The summer-house, or observatory as it was called, had no flaring paint to mar the beauty of the scene, making gaudy attempt to vie with the sunset. It was of the soft gray tint that the wind and the sun and the rain spread over what is left them to paint. The human watchers were, for the most part, silent too, though one of them hummed softly to himself, "More love to thee, O Christ," until it seemed as if the song were a part of the sweet night air, breathing the very words into each heart.

By and by the sky became more muted, and the evening star peeped shyly out, looking around to see if the sun could anywhere be seen, and then glowing more brightly as it gained courage. Soon over the water sounded the tones of the church bell. But it seemed, though sweet and clear, only halfhearted in its call; and it may be that the ringer was at fault, for the sound did not invite joyfully, but slowly told of duty ahead.

"Why, it is prayer meeting night!" said one of the lingerers at the sunset, reluctantly drawing out his watch. Surely, they had all forgotten! But why was it that the thought of the little church did not seem as pleasant as this place where they had felt so near to God? Could it be that, as they went slowly down the hill, with many a lingering look at the fading light, they actually had a thought that God was sending them away to do some disagreeable duty for him?

Be that as it may, it seemed as though they did not all take his Spirit with them as they came straggling by ones and twos into the prayer meeting room. The room itself was not naturally of a cheerful disposition; and its air, from confinement during the week, had become musty and dusty. Whoever acted as sexton seemed not to think it worthwhile to light up much for so few people; for the kerosene lamps, set on brackets very high upon the wall, had to exert themselves as much as their turned-down condition would allow in order to make any light at all through their cloudy chimneys.

There were but two singing books in the room, one on the pulpit and one shut up in the organ. The regular pastor of the church was away, and had asked a brother minister who was there on his vacation to lead in his place. One smoky lamp stood on the desk to glare unflinchingly into his eyes, and make him appear like a dark specter to the people in front who were trying to see him. There were several good musicians there; but the leader did not appear to know it, for he looked despairingly at the vacant organ stool, and then after whispered consultations with one or two near him, who all shook their heads emphatically said, "Is there someone present who will preside at the organ and help in the singing?"

Deep silence ensued. There was a young man near the organ who played in his own church at home. He looked at the instrument and then at the minister, hesitated, looked again, and finally sat still. So did everyone else.

The minister gave out a hymn, carefully announcing twice the number and page, utterly unconscious of the fact that he was the only one in the room who possessed a book. He looked about once more encouragingly, in the hope that someone would appear to play; but as no one did, he said, "Will someone kindly lead us in the singing?" Dead silence again.

A young lady in the audience looked down at her toes, and thought to herself that perhaps she might start the tune if she was perfectly certain no one else would start out at the same time, and come into collision with her. She began thinking the tune over to herself, to see whether it would be too high if she should start; but the thought of it all had made her heart beat so fast that she concluded she should choke and break down if she tried, so she gave over the effort. The minister looked worried. He could not sing himself, poor man, or thought he could not, which served the same purpose. At last, just as he was about to make one more appeal, a dear old sister with a very cracked voice started the tune in a very high key. Such of the congregation as could climb high enough accompanied her, though she had it pretty much her own way through some parts of the verse. The minister noticed the scarcity of the music, and, looking about for a cause, discovered the lack of books. At the close of the hymn he remarked that he was sorry there were no more books, but that they would sing familiar hymns, and try to do their best, if everyone would help.

Now, there sat a boy in that room, who knew that not ten feet away from him was a closet door behind which were a hundred copies just like the singing book which the minister held; and yet he did not stir from his seat to get them. Perhaps he did not think, or the distance from his seat to that door looked very long, or it might be that his boots squeaked, or he did not care about the singing, anyway.

The minister prayed at length in heavy sentences, and not with his usual warmth. The singing had somehow depressed him.

It had been labor instead of praise. After the prayer came the reading of the chapter. There having been no regular topic for the evening announced, he had selected the thirteenth chapter of John, where Jesus talks with his faithful ones about the new commandment of love which he gives to them, which shall be the sign by which all men shall know that they are his disciples. Then they labored with another hymn, after which the leader made some remarks upon the chapter he had read; but the audience seemed to have almost forgotten what it was about, for they listened with a dreamy sort of air that showed their whole minds were not upon the subject.

At the close of a verse of another hymn, the meeting was thrown open for prayer. They all sat as if under a spell, until at last one good old man arose and prayed long and in a low tone, unheard by more than half of those present. The leader had hoped that this would start others: but no; when the old man sat down there ensued a silence more intense than before. "Will someone else lead us in prayer?" he asked with the feeling that a little push would set things going all right. But no one else seemed inclined to pray. There was no help in falling back upon the singing, for each new attempt seemed a worse failure than the last, until it was becoming a positive torture to the poor minister to announce anything. And so the meeting dragged its weary minutes away. Occasionally some one would make a monotonous, commonplace speech, or a prayer whose sentences were old and dead, and asked for nothing in particular; but there were, all the way through, those awful pauses, like yawning chasms, between everything that was said or sung or done.

It was not that they had no thoughts, these people who had brought their bodies without gladness up to the house of the Lord. One of those who had witnessed the sunset sat there, and his mind was filled with the glory of it still. He was thinking how like a Christian's death is the sunset, with its greatest glory and beauty coming at the end of its course. The idea interested him much; and he proceeded to carry it out in his mind, likening the whole course of the sun to the life of a Christian. It did occur to him to tell his thoughts to the meeting, but he could not seem to make anything he had to say fit the subject, and so he sat still; and it was a pity, for there were some there, hardworking people, in whose hearts the "world had been set" so firmly that they had almost forgotten that "He hath made everything beautiful in his time," and that the sunsets were given for them to look at, and from which to learn God's lessons.

There was a girl thinking over to herself with beating heart the words:

I was poor yesterday, but not today;
For Jesus came this morning
And took the poor away;
And he left the legacy
He promised long ago.
So peace and joy and love
Through all my being flow.

I was tired yesterday, but not today.
I could run and not be weary
This blessed way;
For I have his strength to stay me,
With his might my feet are shod,
I can find my resting places
In the promises of God.

What if she should dare to repeat those verses? Perhaps they would not fit, after all, and she was in a strange place. It would be better for her to keep still. Nevertheless, as each painful pause occurred, her heart beat loudly, and told her many times that she was almost on the point of opening her mouth; but she did not.

One old elder talked of the new commandment, the love that ran all through the Bible. Near him sat a young man who was a musician. The week before he had been in Music Hall in his city home, and listened to the wonderful tones of the great pipe organ. Somehow his thoughts were carried back now to that music. He could hear the strains again. There was the deep-toned bass, the plaintive alto, the sweet tenor; but soaring high above all, clear and beautiful, came the soprano. Love was like that soprano, soaring above everything else, uplifting and bearing along. The thought seemed to the young man a good one, and he carried it out more fully; but only for his own benefit. He did not open his mouth for the others to hear. Several brethren had it in their hearts to pray; but when they considered the matter, there really did not seem to be much they could ask for except that the meeting might be blessed. It did not occur to them that they were doing their best to keep it from being a blessing to anyone, and that perhaps it was in their hands to make it a good one. However that was, they kept still.

"For I have loved thee with an everlasting love, therefore with lovingkindness have I drawn thee." These words came to one present; and her heart told her to repeat them, and tell the others how God had verified that promise to her.

"He that hath my commandments, and keepeth them, he it is that loveth me; and he that loveth me shall be loved of my Father, and I will love him, and will manifest myself to him," thought another one of his disciples as she sat quietly in a shadowy corner.

"Behold what manner of love the Father hath bestowed upon us, that we should be called the sons of God." "God is love; and he that dwelleth in love dwelleth in God, and God in him." How the verses multiplied in the hearts of the worshipers! But they did not speak the words aloud.

An old lady during the lengthy pauses longed to call for her favorite hymn:

There's a wideness in God's mercy,
Like the wideness of the sea.
There's a kindness in his justice
Which is more than liberty.

But she remembered the difficulty with which they had sung even those that the leader had selected, and her courage failed

122

her. By her side sat a young lady who could have sung that sweet hymn so that it would have sounded almost like angel music, for she had often done so; but neither of them knew, and so the meeting lost that. One man in the audience remembered the words of an eminent speaker whom he had once heard: "We are Christ's inheritance. What has he in us?" and thought of quoting the verses, "And when they had called the apostles, and beaten them, they commanded that they should not speak in the name of Jesus, and let them go. And they departed from the presence of the council, rejoicing that they were counted worthy to suffer shame for his name," with the added sentence, "That is what Jesus Christ had in those disciples; what has he in us?" He thought the sentences over so many times that they finally came to have very little force, and he concluded that they were better left unsaid. If he had but said those words, it might have roused some few disciples to the fact that they were far from following the example of those who rejoiced to be counted worthy to suffer from speaking "in his name," but were acting just as though someone had really commanded that they should not speak in the name of Jesus. No doubt

Satan had, and they obeyed.

"Do not let the time run to waste," urged the leader; nevertheless, he would have been glad if it had "run" a little faster. Even the dragged-out singing did not take up much of it. Now and then he threw in a remark himself when the pauses were unbearable; but he was growing nervous, and his remarks seemed desultory. He was a young man, and it embarrassed him exceedingly to have a meeting that he led go in this way. It lacked a good ten minutes of the end of the hour when he at last arose and said with a sigh, "Well, if no one has anything to say we will close by singing, 'Nearer my God, to thee.' "

They sang it in the same laborious way they had used for all the other hymns, and the long drawn out, "E'en though it be a cross," floated out from the church to sound to the chance passerby as though the people felt they were bearing that cross then and there, and that it was a heavy one. Then they bowed their heads, almost impatiently waiting for the parting words of blessing, and hastened out with a relieved air, as much as to say, "There! We have accomplished that for another week, and we are glad!"

Now, there had been no infidel in that

meeting to sneer and go out to make fun of the church on account of it; but there were many who were halfhearted Christians, and all needed the help that a good prayer meeting would have given. There was even one soul who was questioning in her own mind whether there was anything desirable in religion, and had come that night with the intention of trying to find out; but before the evening was half over she had forgotten all about her interest in Christ, and was filling her mind with other things. No one else seemed to take any interest in the meeting, why should she?

There were some who needed the organ's story of love; some who needed the sunset's picture, and the verses that might have been repeated, or the songs that might have been sung. Of course there were. Why else should they have been put into the hearts of those present? The dim little cheerless chapel might have been filled with sacred thoughts and wonderful pictures for those of Christ's children who spent their winters in that place, and came up to the house to worship every week; and the old lady who did not quite approve of having an organ in the church would have looked at it in a new way, perhaps, if she had only heard it used as a simple yet beautiful illustration; and ever after she might have listened for its soprano notes, and thought of the wonderful love they have been used to symbolize.

Every soul in that room might have been uplifted if each one had done his part. They had forgotten the words, "Then they that feared the Lord spake often one to another; and the Lord hearkened and heard it, and a book of remembrance was written before him for them that feared the Lord and that thought upon his name."

What did the angels think as they watched? And the Lord hearkening, and hearing so little of what he had given to be said? How indifferent and unloving must his children have seemed that night! And the records of that meeting, could they have been written in that wonderful "book of remembrance"?

The Pledge

A new assistant pastor came to the church on the avenue. He had progressive ideas and a brisk business manner, and the people hoped much from his coming. The dear old pastor was beloved by all, and was in hearty sympathy with new ideas that the young people might bring forward; but his eye was dim and his energy abated, and he was not able to give them the active service that they needed. So they looked to the vigorous younger man for help. The Young People's Society of Christian Endeavor was not in the most flourishing condition, and the few faithful workers who were determined that it should not die went to the younger pastor for advice. They looked to see his face kindle with the light of enthusiasm; but instead he looked at them rather coldly, and said, "Well, the fact is, my young friends, I don't believe in the Christian Endeavor Society. In the first place, I do not believe in pledges."

He launched into a long dissertation

upon the evils of pledges; but the faithful few heard little of it. They looked into his face with surprise, and turned away with a sigh, feeling that in him they would find no helper to bring their pledge-breakers back into the fold.

"How is it that he believes in marriage, then?" asked one young woman, as they walked away sadly together. "He had to pledge his truth and honor and love."

"Or how can he urge people to unite with God's church, since they have to take such solemn vows upon themselves?" said the serious one, with troubled eyes.

"He can't do much business with such ideas," said the bright-faced boy, who always forgot to be respectful; "for how could he sign his name to a check? A check is a promise to pay."

"And what more is our Christian Endeavor pledge than a promise to pay to our God what we owe him?" added the serious one.

"Oh, he doesn't understand yet," gently put in the excuser, who always labored painfully to think the best of everyone, especially a minister of God. "The time will come when he will see."

This seemed like a prophecy. Then they sighed for the one that was gone forever from their midst, for they knew what she would have said just here, "We must pray"; and with one accord they went silently into a vacant Bible-class room, and knelt together, their hearts full of petition for help from the Fountainhead.

But since the society, though feeble, was already in existence, and was favored by the senior pastor, and since the pledges already made had been made to God and not to man, the society could not cease to exist. A meeting was called by the faithful few, which the senior pastor promised to attend; and, as there had been special effort made, nearly all whose names had ever been upon the society roll were present, as well as many who had never attended the meetings.

The president made an earnest little speech, an exhortation to the pledge-breakers to renew their vows, and to outsiders to join them. He gave opportunity for others to speak; and after a few minutes' silence a young man arose, and said that he had not joined the society because of the pledge, that he did not believe in pledges; but if they would do away with that feature of their organization, he would be glad to lend them his influence.

The kind eyes of the old pastor had kindled with righteous indignation during this speech; and when it was done he arose and said, "Dear friends, the young brother who has just spoken forgets that it makes very little difference what he believes in the matter, so long as the covenant-keeping God believes in pledges. The pledge is an institution that God has set up, and no man has a right to say he does not believe in it. Has God not promised to send his floods no more upon our earth, and set his rainbow signature to the pledge written across his heavens? Away back in the beginning of the ages God began his pledges; and long years afterward Paul, writing to the Galatians about it, said that even the law could not break the covenant which had been confirmed before of God, to make the promise of none effect."

In the silence that followed these impressively spoken sentences came the clear voice of the student member of the faithful few.

"I was noticing today," said he, "the theological definition of the word 'covenant.' It is this: 'The promises of God as revealed in the Scriptures, conditioned on certain terms on the part of man, as obedience, repentance, faith, etc.' So, then, a covenant, in distinction from a mere promise, implies a condition, and indicates that both parties are concerned in the keeping of it. It seems to me that the first sentence of our Christian Endeavor pledge gives it the nature of a covenant, 'Trusting in the Lord Jesus Christ for strength.' We do not make this pledge alone; it is not a promise to God that we will do certain things for his benefit, but rather an acceptance of his promise to give us strength to do his will. Our pledge then merely states the conditions we must fulfill in order to understand that will. Am I right, doctor?" and he turned loving eyes to his elder pastor's face as he sat down.

"Exactly so, my dear boy," said the old minister, as he rose again. "In signing your names to this pledge you merely do as Jacob did when he rose up and took a vow upon himself that he would do as God had told him to do, if God would keep his covenant. Even as Jacob set up the rock for a memorial to the mutual promise, so do you sign your names to these small white cards, which may have cost some of you wakeful nights, as Jacob's stone pillow cost him. More than this" — and as he spoke the voice of the old Christian veteran seemed to soften and grow tremulous — "there may be some of you who do not know that the supper of our Lord, the sign, the seal, the center of our religion, is, first of all, a covenant, a pledge. You know we call it the sacrament. Do you know the word is derived from the Latin *sacramentum?* And the *sacramentum* was the oath of allegiance of the Roman soldiers. When a new legion had been enlisted, it was the custom to perform the solemn ceremony of taking the *sacramentum.* A shield was taken, upturned, and into it were poured a few drops of the blood of each soldier and of their commander, which was collected from a slight gash made in the bared arm of each by his own sword. Then the shield was held aloft by the commander, and the soldiers passed by in turn, each one as he passed dipping his hand into the blood with the commander. By so doing captain and soldier swore fealty each to the other by this solemn symbol, the captain promising to stand by the soldier, and the soldier by the captain, even to the shedding of the last drop of blood. It was this spirit that made the Roman legion the finest military organization the world has ever seen. It is this spirit that breathes through every part of the communion, the sacrament. Dear young fellow-soldiers, never forget that the communion means the renewal of Christ's vow to you as well as yours to him. Without this, my sixty-seven years of service in Christ's cause could not have been. With this spirit, I pray, I believe, that the Christian Endeavor army, setting it forth so clearly as is done in their pledge, will recruit a legion before whose endurance and devotion to their Master the devotion and endurance of the famed Roman legion will pale. This is my idea of the purpose and the effect of the Christian Endeavor pledge." So saying, he sat down.

There was a hush over the meeting. The young man who had objected to pledges shrank into a small space behind a pillar, and tried to look careless while he read the hymnbook. The others were taking in for the first time the solemnity of their covenant vows. Some drew out their cards and read them, while others' eyes sought the large wall-roll containing, in clear lettering, the pledge. At last a conscientious one spoke.

"Mr. President," he said, "the pledge has always seemed a solemn thing to me, but I have objected to signing because it seemed to me I could not always be sure of keeping my promise. It is too much to promise that I will do whatever Christ would have me do, for how can I be sure in every case just what it is that he would have me do? And then those two things that follow — praying and reading the Bible every day. I do not like to promise that; for I might forget it some time, or there might be occasions or circumstances when it might be impossible. For instance, I have frequently come home from work quite late at night, when my evident duty was to go immediately to rest without taking time for protracted devotions. And what if one were traveling, detained on the road overnight, without a Bible? Or there might be many other circumstances under which one would be compelled to break such a promise. I do not like to promise something that I am not sure I can keep."

Then arose the earnest-faced secretary, who had always a ready answer.

"Mr. President, it seems to me that the rules of daily Bible reading and prayer, together with that first clause, 'Trusting in the Lord Jesus Christ for strength,' are for the purpose of helping us to know and decide under all circumstances just what Jesus Christ would have us do. If we ask his guidance, and read his Word, which is a lamp to light our way, and trust the Spirit to lead, how can we mistake the way that he would have us take? And if we remember the clause, 'I will make it the rule of my life,' which precedes the promise concerning the prayer and Bible reading, the tenderest conscience need not be afraid to promise."

"And I want to say," added a frank-faced member of the faithful few, "that I objected to signing the pledge once on that account. I said I was afraid I couldn't always get time to read the Bible; but I found out on looking into my heart that the true reason was that I did not want to tie myself to reading every day. Then I signed the card. I keep it in the frame of my dressing-case mirror, where I see it whenever I enter my room. I want to say right here that I have discovered one benefit of the pledge-card; many a time it has reminded me, and I have opened my Bible just because I promised, when otherwise I would have thought myself too tired or too busy to read, and I've found the bit of comfort, or rest, or admonition, that I exactly needed. I don't believe anyone is ever too tired or too busy to read at least one verse in the Bible every day, and he will surely find himself better off for doing so. It seems to me in these days of cheap Bibles that every Christian might have a small Bible or a piece of one in his pocket, so that it wouldn't be possible for us to get caught anywhere unable to keep that part of our pledge."

"The only thing I object to in the pledge," said a constitutional objector, "is the part about the regular church services. Of course I'll go to church when I can; and it seems to me an utterly unnecessary cumbering of the pledge. I must say if I go to the Christian Endeavor meeting, I consider I have done my duty, and I don't feel bound to go out to the Wednesday evening church prayer meeting, nor to stay to evening preaching Sunday if I want to go home. The fact is, I can't conscientiously spare so much time to meetings."

This brought the dear old pastor to his feet again.

"Children," he said, "dear children, now right here let me warn you. Don't make a mistake. The greatest argument that has ever been urged against the Christian Endeavor movement is that it draws the young people away from the church prayer meetings and regular church services, and that their hearts are enlisted merely for their society, and not for the church of Christ. Take care. That is right against the Christian Endeavor principles. Your motto is, 'For Christ and the Church.' What is your organization for, if not to do better work for and in the church? And how can you do it if you, who are to be its future members and pastors and leaders, go away from its meetings, and leave us poor old folks, who are almost ready to leave the church on earth for the one in heaven, to run all the meetings? We need you in our prayer meetings, and we need you in the church services, both morning and evening. Bring your short prayers and verses and speeches into the church prayer meeting, and help us old ones to be young. Bring your fresh, earnest faces to the evening service, to encourage the pastor as he preaches, and to help us to draw in outsiders. You can always conscientiously give that as a reason to your heavenly Father for absenting yourself from your own meetings."

"But these excuses," said another. "I'm not always willing to give to the world my reason for being away from meeting, and I don't like the idea of pledging to speak in meeting always. It makes the speaking or praying merely perfunctory. Why not leave that out, and let us take part when we have something to say?"

Said the chairman of the prayer meeting committee: "But how could we keep up the interest in our meetings if we were not sure the members would all be present, and would be sure to take some part? There would be times when no one would feel like saying anything; and if the pledge was taken away, many of the members would cease to make preparation before meeting. The excuse is but a help, after all, making the members and the meeting feel that they are in sympathy, even if they are not all able to be in one room at the meeting."

There was much discussion before this meeting finally broke up; but at its close many pledgebreakers came forward and re-signed the pledge, and others, who had never been interested before, came, asked for pledgecards, and went home thoughtfully studying them.

The result was that in a few weeks the membership roll of the society had largely increased, the attendance was trebled, and there were added interest and solemnity in the meetings. The next week's Wednesday evening prayer meeting felt the change. Many young faces were there, and several young voices timidly broke the pauses which had hitherto been so painful. The weeks that succeeded proved that this was not a momentary prick of conscience which had been given to the society. The members took it upon themselves to see that there was a large delegation always at the church prayer meeting, and they urged upon every possible occasion the supremacy of the church service over their own society meeting. No more went the society trooping home or out to take a pleasant walk Sunday evening, instead of going into the church after their prayer meeting. It gladdened the hearts of both pastors to see the large audiences; and outsiders began to wonder what were the attractions in that church, and to come and see.

Nor was this all. Even the new assistant pastor had to acknowledge a spirit of willingness to help on the part of all his young people; and just about a year from that time his faithful few had that talk with him about the pledge, he gathered them all in a group about him after a sweet Sunday's work was done, and told them: "Dear friends, I want to take back what I said a year ago, for I have learned better things. I do believe in the Young People's Society of Christian Endeavor; and I do believe, for I have been made to see the value of it, in its pledge."

A Missionary Meeting

"What's the subject of our meeting to-night, Tom?" asked Cousin Helen one Sunday afternoon. "I've lost my topic card, and could not remember what was given out in church this morning; so I ran in here to see yours."

"It's an old missionary meeting," answered Tom, throwing down the paper he had been reading. "I wish it was anything else."

"Why, Tom Brainard! Aren't you ashamed of yourself?" said Helen, laughing at the expression on his face.

"I don't know as I am," answered Tom. "Sit down, Helen. I've been bothered about this ever since church was out. You see, Fred Millard is sick. It was his turn to lead; and he has sent word to me to lead it, and I can't find a thing on earth to make it go. You can't make a missionary meeting interesting, anyway. Just think back, Helen; we've never had one interesting missionary meeting in all the time our society has been organized, have we?"

"No," admitted Helen, after a moment's sober thought. "I don't know that we have."

"Well, just see; here it is the time of year when there'll be a good many strangers from the hotel present — that is, if our hotel committee has done its work well — and there ought to be a meeting that will do them good. We have grand ones when we have any other topic, but a missionary meeting just kills us dead. There'll be nothing but dry statistics, and every stranger that comes in will wish he had stayed at home. I don't know how to manage it, I'm sure. Dr. Brower will get up and read a long article from some magazine; and who will know any more when he is done than when he began? Then we'll sing 'From Greenland's Icy Mountains,' and 'Rescue the Perishing,' and there will be some more statistics read by Fannie Moore and Miss Van Anden, and then the meeting will drag. And what I'm to do for my part of it I'm sure I don't know"; and Tom slid down a little farther in his easy chair, and scowled.

Helen laughed at his description; but she felt that it was perfectly true.

"They are boring, that's a fact, Tom — or rather, always have been," she said; "but

I don't see why they should be. If missionary meetings are good things to have — and I suppose they must be, or they would not be upheld by all the good people in the church, and urged so much by the head of our society — why, then there must be some way to make them interesting."

"I should like to know what it is," said Tom.

"How nice it would be if we only had a real missionary with us to talk about missions, wouldn't it?" said Helen thoughtfully.

"I don't know," said Tom gloomily; "we haven't, anyway, so what's the use? And if we had, he would be likely to tell just as many statistics as Dr. Brower will read. Besides, that wouldn't be what I should call a Christian Endeavor missionary prayer meeting. That would be more like a lecture, or an amusement for us, if it was at all interesting."

"That is true," answered Helen. "Well, if missionary work is one of the things that we as Christians ought to have to do with, and to help along in, why shouldn't we be interested in it as well as in any other subject?"

"Well, we aren't," said Tom almost crossly; "and I don't see how we are to get up an interest, I'm sure. As for professing to be interested in those long articles full of strange names of places and people, I can't say I am, and that's all there is about it. I never feel as if I had received a bit of good from them. I only wish *you* had to lead this meeting."

"Well, I don't," answered Helen, laughing, "for I should be as much at a loss as you are; but, Tom," and her face sobered, "have you been to the Head for orders?"

"What do you mean?" asked her cousin, with a puzzled expression.

"Why," said Helen, her cheeks growing a little pink, and hesitating, she hardly knew why, to speak what she had to say, "I mean, have you prayed about it?" She looked down in her lap, and fingered the corner of her handkerchief. These two cousins were used to talking about their society and all that pertained to it, but had always felt a little shy of speaking plainly about what was most dear to them. They lived next door to one another, and were dear companions on all occasions; but it was a little hard for Helen to say what she did.

Tom looked at her in surprise for a minute, and then laughed in a rather embarrassed way.

"No, I don't know as I have," he answered; "but what — well — what good would that do? God has given me brains; doesn't he expect me to do the best I can with them?"

"O Tom, you know better than that. You know he has told you to ask his help always; and hasn't he promised to even give words when they are needed? Why, it's his meeting, Tom, not yours; and he certainly doesn't want it to be an uninteresting one. He would like to have it reach the hotel strangers as much as you would. You ask him now, and I will run home and pray about it too"; and she started toward the door.

"No, wait, Helen!" he said, rising quickly, and catching her hand to detain her. "You stay here and pray. Let us pray together. We are not afraid of each other; and we can claim the promise that 'If two of you shall agree on earth as touching anything that they shall ask, it shall be done,' you know"; and he led her over to the sofa, where they both knelt and opened their hearts to God about the meeting that night.

As they arose, Tom said, "Now, Helen, you must stay and help me get ready," and so through the Sunday afternoon they studied. Papers and books were brought out; the missionary news columns were carefully looked over. The two young people grew quite excited over their work as the time went by and the hour of the meeting drew nearer.

"My, I wish I had a whole week to get ready in!" exclaimed Tom at last, as he threw down the pile of papers he had been looking through, and reached over to the table for his Bible.

"But you have enough items now that are interesting, Tom," said his cousin.

"Yes, enough, perhaps," admitted Tom; "but I would have liked to give them out to the members early in the week, and they would have been thinking about it, and have had a little word ready to add. It would have been a great deal better."

"And some of them would have been praying for the success of the meeting, too, perhaps, if their special attention had been called to it," added Helen gently.

"Perhaps," said Tom, "and, after all, that's the secret of a good meeting. But we must have some Bible now," and he plunged into his study of that. What a whirl he felt himself in then! There was enough Bible on the subject of missions to supply material for unnumbered meetings.

Tom began to wonder why he had never discovered it before. What theme should he take? The thought of Christian giving? Shining as lights in a dark world? Witnessing for Christ? Helping Christ's kingdom to come? There were verses and verses, and they all rushed in upon him at once, and bewildered him.

"Helen," he said in desperation, "there won't be time for any items from the papers, as far as I can see; the Bible has too much to say about it. I had no idea this subject was so rich."

Helen looked up with flushed cheeks and shining eyes.

"O Tom! isn't it grand? We might have a missionary meeting every week for a year, and then not exhaust the subject. We shall just have to go over these bits we have cut from the paper, and drop out all but two or three of the very best, and that will leave room for more Bible."

"Yes; but Helen, what shall I do about selecting a passage to read? If I begin, I can't find a place to stop."

"Take the grandest one you can find, the one that will suggest the greatest number of other passages, and at the same time be the one that others would be the least likely to select," answered Helen.

The twilight found them still at work, but with more hopeful hearts than at first. A very few slips of neatly written paper represented their work that afternoon. On the papers were some items of interest concerning mission work, and a few carefully selected texts of Scripture, which the careless searcher would not be likely to find, these to be handed to one or two timid members who never knew what to say, especially on the subject of missions. Helen and Tom had planned just which ones they should be handed to, and had made the most of the talents of the people they knew would probably attend the meeting.

"There's Albert," said Tom. "No need to hand him anything; he'll be sure to have something good to say, even if the subject of the meeting should be, 'How to build church steeples.'"

"Yes," said Helen, "and so will Mary Elder; and I sometimes think that those two help more than any other two in our society, because what they say always makes one feel as if they lived very near to Jesus."

By and by the bell began to toll, and Tom and Helen walked down the street toward the church side by side. They were quiet now. They had just come from their own rooms, where each had spent a few minutes in earnest prayer for a blessing on the meeting; and as they entered the pleasant chapel, they breathed one more word of petition.

The room was filling rapidly already, and many strangers were among the number. The town was a small winter resort in the South, and this was the season of year when tourists were most numerous.

"Oh, isn't it just an awful pity that this is a missionary meeting?" whispered Clara Horton to another earnest follower of Jesus Christ. "Just see all these strangers, and they will be sure not to be interested. There goes that man who came in a private car three days ago. He stops at the hotel, and is very rich. They say he scarcely ever goes to church. I wonder what brought him. I didn't think the hotel committee would hardly dare send one of their invitations to him. He looks scornful. I just know he'll make all sorts of fun. It's too bad that it isn't a consecration meeting, or anything else but missionary night."

"Yes, it is a pity," assented her friend, glancing in the direction of the haughty looking, handsome old man who had been seated well up toward the front. "It's strange that he cared to come to a young people's meeting, isn't it? What a pity he couldn't have been here last week! We had such a good meeting then!"

The meeting was opened by singing; and the children of the heavenly Father who supposed themselves so wise stopped whispering to sing,

"There's a work for me, and a work
 for you,
Something for each of us now to do."

They sung the words without thinking much what they were. It was an old hymn. Tom had hesitated when he selected it, but it seemed to fit so entirely into his thoughts that he could not but use it. His prayer that followed the hymn was one of personal consecration and of earnest pleading for the presence of Jesus in the room that evening; and the sharp old man eyed the young leader intently as he gave out another hymn, "One More Day's Work for Jesus," and sat down to turn over the leaves of his Bible a moment.

Tom read only two verses, after all, from the many that he had found. They were these: "The God of our fathers hath chosen thee, that thou shouldest know his will, and see that just One, and shouldest hear the voice of his mouth. For thou shalt be his witness unto all men of what thou hast seen and heard."

He said but few words himself. His thought was that each one of the members of that society was chosen of God as a missionary to do some special work, even though it might be but small.

"I have asked Miss Gladden to sing us an old song that illustrates this thought," he said in conclusion, as he nodded to the young lady at the organ.

It was not a wonderful voice that sang the words; but it was sweet and clear, and every word was spoken with a distinctness that brought it home to each heart listening:

"Hark, the voice of Jesus calling,
'Who will go and work today?'"

The sharp eyes of the old man watched the singer's face as she sang, and he cleared his throat several times at the close. The room was very still, hushed by the thought of the song, when Tom said, "Let us have a good many short prayers. John Raymond, will you lead us?" and immediately every head was bowed.

Oh, they were earnest Christians, every

one of them, only they were not used to carrying their consecration into their missionary meetings. But now every heart was lifted up for a blessing, and they had all forgotten that this was a missionary meeting. There followed in quick succession many heartfelt sentences of pleading for blessing, of earnest consecration, and some even breathing the spirit of the answer to the Master's call, "Here am I, Lord; send me, if thou hast aught for me to do."

"Let us sing one verse," said Tom, when there came a pause, and they sang:

"If once all the lamps that are lighted
Should steadily blaze in a line,
Wide over the land and the ocean,
What a girdle of glory would shine!
How all the dark places would brighten!
How the mists would roll up and away!
How the earth would laugh out in
*   her gladness,*
To hail the millennial day!
Say, is your lamp burning, my brother?
I pray you, look quickly and see;
For if it were burning, then surely
Some beam would fall brightly on me."

"The verse that we have just sung," said

151

a young girl, "reminds me of what a returned missionary once told me. She said that she had always taught her little girl, who had been born in Turkey, and who had never been to this country, that America was a Christian land; and the little girl, without her knowledge, had formed the idea that everyone who lived here belonged to Jesus Christ and served him. When they brought her here she was about seven years old. One day her mother took her out in the street of a city, and in passing some men she heard them swear. The little girl stood looking after them sorrowfully, and then said to her mother, 'Mamma, I feel sick.' Her mother took her home as quickly as possible, and after she felt better questioned her as to what had happened that made her feel so ill all in a minute; for the mother thought her symptoms indicated that she had had a shock of some sort. 'Oh, Mamma,' she answered, 'you told me this was a Christian land, where everybody loved Jesus; and I heard some men use God's name in the way the bad men over in Turkey used to do.' The little trusting heart had evidently been shocked by finding that in this land where everyone knows about Jesus, not all were followers of him. If we would only, all of us whose lamps are lighted, go to work and keep our lights bright, might we not make a difference in this country, so that when those from lands that do not honor our God come over here, they will find that this is truly a Christian land? There is indeed much work left here for missionaries to do."

"I have been thinking," said one of the young men, standing up and facing the roomful of people, "while the sweet song was being sung to us, of Miss Havergal's poem:

> *In God's great field of labor*
> *All work is not the same;*
> *He hath a service for each one*
> *Who loves his holy name.*
> *And you to whom the secrets*
> *Of all sweet sounds are known,*
> *Rise up, for he hath called you*
> *To a mission of your own."*

Said Helen: "I have been interested in reading about a Christian Endeavor Society in a foreign land. It is in a mission boarding school, and is formed of young men and women who have known Jesus Christ but a short time, most of them. They are very poor, as the mission board can appropriate but little to the needs of the school; and there are constantly scholars wishing to enter the school who cannot be allowed to do so, because there is no money to pay for even the barest necessities of life. The boys of the school go out to sell papers and such things on Saturdays, and so are able to earn a few cents to help along; but in that country it would be a disgrace for the girls to do the same, so they have very few ways of earning any money for themselves.

"There came a young man to the school one day, a friend of some of the other students, and begged to be allowed to enter as a pupil; but the teachers sadly shook their heads, saying, 'We cannot allow it. We have no money to feed you, and nothing with which to buy books for you, and we cannot afford to let you enter without paying the small tuition that is necessary to keep the school running.' The young man turned sadly away; but some of the scholars got together and talked it over, and it was brought up in their Christian Endeavor meeting. The result was that the whole society went to the teachers, and said, 'We have decided that we will give up our meat on Fridays [they were so poor they could afford to have meat but once a week] if you will take the money that buys the meat for us, and use it toward paying for this poor boy who wants to learn about Jesus Christ.' They were allowed to do so. Then the boys each gave what money they could earn in selling their papers, gladly sacrificing the little comforts they had been able thus to procure for themselves.

"But the girls said, 'What can we do? We cannot go out to sell things.' They got together and talked the matter over, and decided that they would go without their meals on one day out of every week if the money that supplied the table for that day could be used for the poor boy. It seemed to me, after reading that true story, that we in our society know nothing at all about sacrificing for missions, that those poor Christians have gone way ahead of us. If they can do so much, shall we hesitate over giving up some luxury?"

This seemed to touch many hearts, and brought out other items and thoughts.

"Ye have not chosen me, but I have chosen you, and ordained you, that ye should go and bring forth fruit, and that your fruit should remain: that whatsoever ye shall ask of the Father in my name, he may give it you," recited another member, adding, "My heavenly Father has frequently comforted me with that verse, reminding me that it is not my work, after all, that I am doing, but his, for which he has chosen me, and that however dark the way may seem, and however my plans may have come to naught, yet I have ever the assurance that the fruit shall remain; and, with that promise that whatever I shall ask of the Father shall be given, why need I doubt and grow discomfited when my plans for doing his work seem for a time to fail? I want, as my blessing from this meeting, to get more faith in his service, and less trust in myself."

When the hour was over it was a surprise to all.

"We have had a good meeting!" exclaimed one and another, as they looked into each other's astonished eyes at the close, and shook hands with the warm clasp that they always used when their hearts had been touched.

But it was the haughty old man in the front seat who gave the final surprise to the little society, and started its enthusiasm for a new era of missionary meetings. He stepped up to Tom as soon as the benediction had been repeated, and laid his hand on Tom's shoulder, while the other hand gave that amazed young man a roll of bills.

"Give that to your treasurer for the missionary cause," he said, and hastened away before Tom had time to frame fit words of thanks.

Fifty dollars all at once to go into their missionary fund! It was more than this little society had dreamed of giving for years yet. They were poor, and for the most part the money came in slowly and in very small quantities. They gathered in a group about Tom, looking with reverence at the bills. It seemed to them a material sign that the Lord had truly been with them that night and blessed them; and those few who always stayed a few moments to talk things over after the others were gone, went home with the feeling that they could never have another cold, dry, statistical missionary meeting again.

"Helen," said Tom, as he reached out his hand to relieve her of her Bible and hymnbook, on their way home, "this has been a wonderful evening for me, and I believe it is all a credit to you. The Lord put it into your heart to suggest the praying. I do believe that has been the matter with all our meetings. There has not been enough of prayer — beforehand and during the meeting, too. I mean to do differently about that hereafter. That is the secret of success in Christian work, after all. It has helped us all this time, and I shouldn't wonder at all if the old man felt that he had a blessing, too. Prayer is a wonderful thing!"

Some Carols for the Lord

Half a dozen young people were on their way home from a Christian Endeavor social when the idea was first mentioned, and this was how it began.

"What are we going to do for Christmas as a society?" asked Jessie. "I wish we could think of something new and delightful."

"So do I," chimed in Kitty. "We have never done anything but just join with the Sunday school in having a Christmas tree. I'm tired of trees, for my part, though I suppose the little children like them. But there is such a lot of work, and not much to show for it afterward. We get all tired out fixing dolls, and deciding which child shall have a book, or which ought to have a ball. Then the children are often disappointed at what they receive, and the church is covered with popcorn and mashed candies, and you can't go there to service for a week or two afterward without finding an old nut or a gumdrop hiding somewhere under your seat, no matter how hard you sweep. I worked like a slave for three hours last year, helping to sweep the church the day afterward, and then kept finding stray candies and bits of gold paper for a month."

"You might have a fishpond," suggested Fred Hall.

"O Fred, don't!" groaned Jessie. "We want something new that we've never tried before. Fishponds are as old as the hills; and so are old women who lived in a shoe, and had so many children they didn't know what to do. Besides, I never did think those things were suitable for the church; and they make as much mess and work, and aren't nearly so dignified as a tree."

"I'm squelched, Jessie," laughed Fred; "and I retire from making any further suggestions."

"I wish we had the custom of singing Christmas carols in this country; I think it is so pretty," said Myrtle Brown.

"That's an idea!" exclaimed Jessie. "We might sing some. Wouldn't that be interesting?"

"I should like to know if that isn't 'old as the hills,' as you termed it, madam?" said Fred.

They all laughed, of course, and tried to explain to Fred the difference; and when the hubbub had somewhat subsided, Myrtle put in again, "We tried it once on a small scale, my three cousins and I. We were up in the country for the holidays; and we stole out of the house before anyone was awake, when it was scarcely light, and sang under the windows. It was a great deal of fun, and they said it sounded very sweet. I should think it might do good if we chose the right carols."

"It's just the thing!" exclaimed Jessie. "Let's do it. We could have two or three bands of singers, and divide the town, each band taking a district. I've heard of great good done through singing. We might reach some in that way that we have not been able to reach in any other. Who are we here, anyway? I'm chairman of the social committee; I shouldn't wonder if such things came among our duties. Myrtle, you and Kittie and Frank are all 'socials.' We're all here but Truman. Harold, you're chairman of the Sunday school committee, aren't you? And Fred —"

"Only your humble president," put in Fred before Jessie could finish, "and I'll try to forget my feelings and do anything that's expected of me."

They grew very eager with their laughing and talking. All were agreed that the plan was at least interesting. Each knew some pretty carol that he would like to have sung, and each had some suggestion.

"What'll you do with all the money we've been putting aside for a Christmas entertainment? You know we decided last Christmas to save some each month for Christmas, so that when the time came we would not have to run all over town, and use the children's collections, which they had been supposed to give for the heathen, in order to buy them dolls and kites and books and things. I shouldn't wonder if the youngsters would be disappointed too." This was Harold's contribution to the conversation.

"We might take the presents along, and tie them to the doorknobs," suggested Frank.

"That's a good thought," said Jessie, amid the laughter that followed this proposal.

"But, Jessie," said Myrtle, "we couldn't get enough things to go around, and some would be disappointed."

"Why, Myrtle, I'm not so sure of that," she responded seriously. "It wouldn't do for us to sing under the windows of any but our own church people, or of those who belonged to no church, and are not being got hold of by any other, because the

162

other two churches would be sure to think we were proselyting. I should think we might get together enough things to go respectably around among the people who legitimately belong to our society. I don't mean members merely of the society and church, but people whom we ought to be able to get hold of, and have not been able to reach heretofore. We could at least leave a Christmas card at each door."

"That would be beautiful; but we should have to keep it a grand secret from those we were to sing to," said Myrtle.

"Let's go in and see if Dr. Clifton likes the idea. We can't do anything without his approval, and I can't wait until morning. I want to dream out more plans," said Jessie. "Isn't it good that the social was so far away tonight? We have things in really quite a presentable shape to talk about."

"I'm afraid it's too late tonight, Jessie," suggested Kitty prudently. But just then they came to the pastor's gate, and found him standing there himself, bidding good night to a gentleman.

"O Dr. Clifton! May we come in and tell you a new plan, and see if it's worth anything? It will not take long, and we can hardly wait till morning," exclaimed Jessie eagerly.

"Certainly, certainly; come in, friends. I shall be only too glad to hear it. I can't wait until morning myself; I'm all curiosity," said the genial old minister.

Of course he approved the plan; and it was with faces full of a delightful secret that they once more took their way home.

It was near the last of November, and there were many things to be done; but the workers were all eagerness. The president called a meeting of the society in haste, and stated to them that the social committee had a plan for Christmas which, in order to be carried out to perfection, must be kept a secret from all except those whom they should call to their aid. He further said that the pastor knew and approved it, and that the committee would like to be authorized to go forward and carry out their plans. The chairman of the committee then stated that a part of their plan was to have the usual amount of money spent in gifts, and that they should like to be allowed to use the sum that had been set apart for that purpose.

The question having been carried by vote, the chairman said that they should need the assistance of every member in the carrying out of their project, and that, as they wanted to begin work at once, they

164

would ask the following members to go to the different Bible-class rooms as they were called. He then read the names in groups of five, six, or seven, assigning each group to a separate classroom of the church. Each one of these groups was presided over by someone who had previously been instructed. All were soon at work. The strictest secrecy was enjoined upon the carolers, who commenced practicing at once.

The social committee, with a few others, had worked hard before this meeting, planning which members should be in the different groups, and dividing the town into districts, that no time might be lost if their plan was accepted. There was much to be done yet. A large calling committee was started around to ascertain the number of people in each house that they intended visiting, their ages, tastes, needs, and desires. They were to use every means possible to find out in what way they could make most useful the little money they had to spend.

The pastor announced that the Christian Endeavor Society was preparing for a celebration at Christmas time, and would be glad of contributions of turkeys, vegetables, groceries, dry goods, toys, or anything that usually goes to make up Christmas festivities; and that for the convenience of the contributors they would be visited by the committee some time during the week.

The committees themselves were not to be told in what way the gifts were to be distributed until Christmas Eve. They rather enjoyed the mystery that hung about the affair; and matters went on more smoothly than they had ever gone before, because everyone, except the social committee, was in such absolutely blissful ignorance, that none could venture to demur at what was to be done and want it to be different.

It had been arranged that on Christmas evening there should be a Christmas service held in the church. This being generally known, it was supposed that any festivities of the occasion would take place at that time; and so the mind of the town was soothed to rest about the matter. The character of this meeting was not known exactly. That had been placed in the hands of others.

The time flew fast, as it always does when people have more than they know how to do. The night before Christmas arrived at last, and all the work was done. Baskets ticketed with the names of many people stood groaning with their heavy loads. There were turkeys and chickens and geese, rabbits and birds and beef; there were potatoes, Irish and sweet, cabbages, celery, cranberries, jellies, all the long list of things that make the best kind of a Christmas dinner. There were warm stockings and flannels and shawls, dress goods, some plain bits of finery, neat and pretty; toys, books, candy, nuts, popcorn, and Christmas cards. You could hardly mention a thing that ever has to do with Christmas that had not its representative in one of those baskets. The committees went to their beds tired, but with happy hearts. They had been told the secret of the whole plan the night before; and with sealed lips and dancing eyes each one went home rejoicing.

Several members were so burdened with the weight of their new secret that they were unable to sleep, and startled their respective families by lighting matches through the night, to see whether it was time to arise and begin. But nearly all the anxious parents were quieted to sleep at last; and the beautiful, sparkling Christmas Eve peacefully hastened its course, till at last the glittering stars, with their memories of a night long ago, began to pale, and the least faint streak of the Christmas morning appeared in the east.

Then those young people arose in haste, and, cautiously donning the apparel that they had been careful to put in a convenient place the night before, slipped down the stairs, and out of their several doors, holding in their hands, and munching on the way, the crackers that the leaders of the various choirs had insisted should be eaten before the work of the morning, or more strictly of the dawning, should be begun. It had been agreed that if any were late they should not be waited for, but the company should proceed to business exactly at the hour intended, and those who were late could follow and join them; but so eager were all these workers for the morning to come, that there were but two out of the whole number who were late, and those two joined their group before they had finished the first carol.

"Waken, Christian children;
Up, and let us sing
With glad hearts and voices
Of our newborn King;

Up, 'tis meet to welcome
With cheerful lay
Christ, the King of glory,
Born for us today."

The clear voices rang out on the cold morning air, waking the sleepers to a new, glad day, startling some from dreams of sorrows to remember what they had almost forgotten, the true meaning of Christmas Day. While the carolers sang, the committees, made up of those who could not sing (or who thought they could not), deftly selected the turkey, or the dolls, or the Christmas cards, one or all, as the case might be, and tied them fast to the doorknob, making ready for the next house as the singers finished their verse and moved on.

At each house where they sang, in addition to the gifts, a small envelope addressed to the householder was left, containing a cordial invitation to him to attend, with his family, the "Christmas praise service," to be held that evening in the church. At the top of the card was printed, "Peace on earth, good will to men," and below the invitation these words, "For unto you is born this day a Saviour, which is Christ the Lord."

Some poor souls, on hearing the music, really felt for a moment that they must be in heaven, so sweetly did it ring out.

"This is the winter morn
Our Saviour Christ was born,

Who left the realms of endless day
To take our sins away.
Have ye no carol for the Lord,
To sing his love, his love abroad?
Have ye no carol for the Lord,
To sing his love, his love abroad?
Hosanna! From all our hearts we raise,
Hosanna, Hosanna! And make our lives
his praise."

It came to the houses of the rich, as well as the poor, this story sweet and old. There had been no respecting of persons that day. There were dainty cards with sprays of lovely flowers or bits of landscape and a sweet Bible verse for some, and there were a few copies of Professor Drummond's little white books, left where it was thought they might do good. The committee had taken great care in selecting and assigning gifts, and had really shown remarkable tact. There were some large houses where money indeed was adequate, but where love had been lacking long since, and where there had not been a Christmas gift in many a day. The gifts were gratefully received, how gratefully the society never knew in all cases, though they heard much about that Christmas Day in later days and years.

And the meeting that night? Why, of course, not everybody that was invited came, but many did. The church was crowded to overflowing. There was not even standing room left, despite the fact that in the two other churches of the town there were Christmas services at the same hour.

After the meeting had been opened by prayer, and singing of the good old Christmas hymn, "While Shepherds Watched Their Flocks by Night," there were several lovely Christmas solos, an exquisite recitation appropriate to the evening, and the reading of a short, touching story. Then an invitation was given for all to take part in the meeting who felt that they had anything to be thankful for. Five minutes were given to the recitation of Bible verses about the Prince of Peace and King of Glory, and Christmas and praise. How the verses came from all over the house! The strangers looked on in astonishment, some of them taking part. It had not seemed to them that there could be so many wonderful verses in the whole of the Bible. And then, in still more wonder, they bowed their heads and heard from many lips short sentences of prayer filled with praise to God and of pleading for forgiveness and consecration. There was time for a few words of testimony before they closed; and the testimonies came from all over the house again, and especially from those who had been benefited by the visits of the young workers in the morning.

"It's been the best Christmas we ever spent!" exclaimed the young people as they went home, still feeling the pressure of gratitude from many hands. "They'll come again; We know they will."

And they did.

The Praise of Men

It was late, and Nellie Beverly was tired. She didn't feel much like reading her Bible; and yet there in the frame of her mirror, staring at her as she reached out her hand to turn off the gas, was her Christian Endeavor pledge. Its words, "to pray and to read the Bible every day," reminded her now that she had failed to keep her promise for that day, and, indeed, for the week before. The thought arrested her motion, and made her reach, instead, for her Bible that lay on its little stand by the dressing table. It was trying, this pledge, always bringing her up standing with its solemn phrases. She drew her brows together as she opened the Bible at random, intending to catch at a verse anywhere in order to satisfy her conscience. She had been one of those in her society who had objected to the good old iron-clad pledge; and, when she found it was inevitable, had argued for some time that the sentence about Bible-reading should be left out, on the ground that

173

there were often times when it was impossible, or at least very inconvenient, to read the Bible every day, as when one was on a long journey, for instance. When that arrangement had failed, she had even debated with herself as to whether she would sign the pledge at all. It had ended in her finally signing; but the sight of that pledge-card always gave her an uncomfortable feeling lest she might not be living up to her vows.

Why was it that the Bible opened just where it did? She was not in the least superstitious, at least not about religion. There had been occasions, however, when it had marred her pleasure to make one of thirteen at the table, and she never counted the carriages at a funeral, and always took pains to see the new moon over her right shoulder. But she was not looking for any special word to be given that night, as she hurriedly scanned the pages with sleepy eyes to find a verse that looked short.

Her thoughts had been busy, too, even as she opened her Bible, with the occurrences of the evening. She had been taking part in an entertainment arranged by the social committee of their Christian Endeavor Society. Over in one corner of her room now was a large valise, which contained her different costumes and the many little things that it had been necessary for her to carry to the hall. Her parts had been difficult, and she had done well. Every one said so; and, indeed, she knew it herself without being told. She had been obliged to pose for several minutes in a difficult attitude, and had been applauded for the beauty and grace of the position, as well as for the steadiness of nerve and muscle shown. The classical costume she had worn was becoming, and there had been many admiring glances cast at her, in addition to more openly expressed admiration and showers of compliments given her. Mrs. Elihu Barker had offered to take her home in her carriage too; and her handsome young son, who had just returned from a German university, had opened the carriage door, helping her in, and seating himself beside her for the homeward ride. Her eyes shone with pleasure as she thought of his elegant compliments; she even felt a little pity for the other girls who had not enjoyed this distinction. To be sure, young Mr. Barker had sneered somewhat at the Christian Endeavor Society and its prayer meetings, and a few of his jokes and gracefully told stories had verged a little too much on the sacred to be altogether pleasing to this young woman who had named the name of the Lord and called herself his child. Nevertheless, she had laughed, for the jokes were exceedingly funny; and a young man who had spent so many years abroad was not expected to have exactly the same strict views of everything that were held here at home. He was very nice, and he had admired her. Vistas of pleasures seemed opening before her.

But what was this that her eyes were reading? "For they loved the praise of men more than the praise of God." Nellie felt startled as she read the words once more. How very strange for her to have opened to that verse! Did God mean to reprove her? She had been thinking a good deal about herself during the last few weeks; and much time and expense had been put upon her preparations for the entertainment, in order that she might gain this "praise of men." It was true that she had been trying to make the entertainment a success for the sake of the society and to give pleasure to others; but really in her heart these things had been secondary, and her main thought had been, How shall I dress and act and pose and sing so as to excite the greatest amount of admiration? This was a rather ugly verse to pillow her head upon for the night. She liked to sink into sleep with the feeling that she had her heavenly Father's blessing; and this verse gave her an uncomfortable feeling, as if he were not altogether pleased with her. It seemed as if he had spoken the words in her ear. What did the verse mean, anyway? She did not remember ever to have seen it before. Who was it that loved to be praised so much? She read the verse before: "Nevertheless, among the chief rulers also many believed on him; but because of the Pharisees they did not confess him, lest they should be put out of the synagogue; for they loved the praise of men more than the praise of God."

With some impatience she ran her eye down the page to find, if she could, a pleasanter verse; and there, a little farther on, stood out the one that she had read in the prayer meeting last week, outlined in pencil that she might easily distinguish it then: "For I have given you an example, that ye should do as I have done to you."

Somehow the two verses had linked themselves together inseparably. This last one reminded her of how Christ had lived and died for her sake, of how he had borne shame, and how, when he was reviled, he opened not his mouth. The whole Book of Isaiah and all of the Gospels stood up with testimony for him in an instant; and there, on the other hand, was pictured in her mind her own behavior that evening, and all the thoughts and ambitions that had been in her mind. These thoughts did not please her, but she could not avoid them. She tried to argue with herself that she had not been so very wrong or vain, and that Mr. Barker was not a Pharisee, but a member of the church — at least, he had been before he went abroad. But she was obliged to go back to those first verses once more. How would it sound if a Bible of today were to be written, and the stories of the disciples of today were put down? Would this story of her own behavior read something like this, she wondered: "Nellie Beverly also believed on Christ; but because of Harold Barker and his set she did not confess him, lest she should be put out of society; for she loved the praise of men more than the praise of God"?

Nellie shivered at this. She had not intended to read all that into the Bible for her own benefit. Her mind had gone on in spite of her, and put the hateful thought into Bible phraseology. She shut the book hastily, and turned the gas out with a click, kneeling beside her bed, as was her custom. But her face was burning with shame as she hid it in her hands and tried to utter a feeble word or two of prayer.

She had thought but a few minutes before that it would not take her long to be asleep that night; but when she laid her head down, after praying, she could not go to sleep for a long time. She had much thinking to do. She must examine her life, and decide what the future should be. She was suddenly brought face to face with her own vows, solemnly made and carelessly broken, and she was resolved that there should be a change. Now that her eyes were once opened, it took but a few minutes to decide what changes must be made in order that she might have the praise of God rather than the praise of men. God himself seemed almost to speak to her, and to show her clearly what her path ought to have been in the past.

It was on the next day that young Mr. Barker called; and Nellie, with a quiet lifting of her heart in prayer for help that she might be worthy of her high calling, went down to receive him. It gave her a little flutter of pleasure as he handed her a note from his mother, begging her to read it and report her answer to him. The note was gracefully worded, saying that guests from a distant city were to be with them over Sunday, and that Mrs. Barker was desirous that her young friend should meet them; and she wished also that they might hear her voice, which had delighted them all so much the evening before. Would Nellie give them the pleasure of her company at tea on Sunday evening, and do them the favor to bring some of her music with her? It could be something suitable for Sunday, of course.

There was an unmistakable glow of delight in Nellie's eyes as she read this note. She had not expected to be taken right into intimacy in this delightful way by a family who moved in the highest circles of society. She raised her eyes to Harold Barker, who, scarcely giving her time to read the note, had gone on to tell her how delighted his mother was with her voice.

"And you should have heard the praise my uncle gave you, Miss Beverly," he was saying. "He considers your voice really remarkable, and I assure you he is a judge."

Sweet words these were to the girl who had spent so much time and money on her voice. But suddenly, as if a voice had spoken in her ear, came the words, "For they love the praise of men more than the praise of God."

Her face changed quickly. She heard no more of the handsomely turned sentences. All at once she became aware of a silence, following a question that had been asked her. She felt, rather than knew, that the question was with regard to her acceptance of the invitation.

"I am very sorry, Mr. Barker," she stammered out. "It would give me great pleasure to meet your mother's guests, and to sing for them, but it is on Sunday night, you know."

He hastened to assure her that he understood that she was not in the habit of going out on Sunday socially, but this was merely among themselves, very quiet. His mother had spoken of that, and said that she was not sure that Miss Beverly might not have some scruples on that account, and that she would have asked her for some other evening but for the fact that the friends were to leave them early Monday morning, and that all the evenings between this and that were fully occupied with other engagements. His mother was very anxious to have her come, and so, indeed, was he; and he hoped she would waive her objections for that time and come to them.

Nellie was not used to arguing on such subjects. She looked down in troubled silence during this speech, almost ready to yield, when the words of the pledge-card came to her mind as they had looked, framed in her mirror, the night before. Was it the Master's help that was given her through the wording of that pledge-card? She gathered courage, and spoke once more, "Mr. Barker, it is impossible. Our Christian Endeavor meeting comes very soon after the time your mother has named as your tea hour."

"Oh!" said he, "I was not aware that you were a member of that society." There was something in his tone that made Nellie remember all the bright sarcasms of the evening before with regard to the society. "But, really, Miss Beverly," more seriously, "I don't suppose you are bound by iron-clad laws to attend that special meeting, are you? Can you not forgo the pleasures of your society for this once?"

Her cheeks grew still redder as she answered quietly, "I have promised, Mr. Barker; that is one of the pledges we make when we join the society, to attend the prayer meetings. I wish your friends were to be here longer, for I should enjoy meeting them. I am very sorry."

"But are there no conditions, Miss Beverly?" he asked, with an impatient frown on his handsome face. "Surely, you are not bound so hopelessly."

"Yes, there are conditions," she answered with a thoughtful, serious look; "the pledge reads, 'Unless hindered by some reason which I can conscientiously give to my Lord and Master.' Do you think that he would accept my own pleasure as an excuse for my staying away from a meeting when he himself has promised to be there?"

Harold Barker was fairly embarrassed, and did not attempt any answer, but looked at her in utter amazement. Surely, this could not be the same young lady who laughed and joked with him last night! He could not but respect her the more, however. She did not look in the least like an "enthusiast," or a "fanatic," or a "crank," or any of those individuals whom he had scornfully denounced. This was a new type of girl, he decided, or else America had changed greatly during his stay abroad. Could it be possible that this Christian Endeavor Society about which such a furor was being made was the cause of all this?

His call did not last much longer. There was nothing left for him to say upon the subject in which he was interested, and he did not know how to converse easily upon this new topic.

Nellie Beverly sighed a little as she thought of all the pleasures that she had put away from her. Her chance for attending those delightful receptions that Mrs. Barker was said to give was entirely over. Nevertheless, she went about her morning duties with a joy in her heart such as she had not known before. Up in her room once more she read over her pledge-card, and smiled at the last sentence, remembering that the next Sunday was the evening for the regular consecration meeting. More than all other meetings she would not have wished to miss this one. How would it have sounded, thought Nellie, if she had sent word to the society that she was obliged to be away from the meeting in order to take tea with some delightful musical and literary people at Mrs. Barker's?

The next Sunday evening proved to be a beautiful one; and the meeting was a solemn one, in which many pledged anew their lives and all to Christ. When Nellie Beverly's name was called, she read the two verses that had so moved her a few evenings before, and added, "I wish to learn to live for the praise of God, rather than the praise of men."

As she turned to lay aside her hymnbook at the close of the meeting, she saw Harold Barker just behind, watching her intently; and as their eyes met, he gave her a grave, respectful bow.

The Love Gift

Chapter One

"Shells are all very well on a seashore, with white sand about, and a fresh breeze blowing; but in this stuffy little room on the mantelpiece, in a wooden butter dish, and considered in the light of an ornament — *that* is too much! Ugh!"

The exclamation was apparently addressed to a very fat cockroach who stood in the middle of the room watching the new occupant, perhaps to see how he was going to like her. So far he had been well pleased with her appearance. She was small and slight; and though she had a rather determined mouth, she looked as though her foot would not be so very heavy if it should happen to come down upon his head. She had been in to look at the room in the morning, had rented it and gone away; and now, just as the gray, drizzly day was drawing to its close, she had come back to it, taken off her hat and jacket, and thrown them on the bed. It must have been his fixed gaze that attracted her attention, for as soon as she had uttered that last word she gathered up her neat traveling dress and started toward him. Her visitor rose up on his hind legs, and pranced off toward the bed, keeping one eye upon her feet all the time, however. She was quick-motioned, and stooped to strike him under the edge of the bed; but by the time her eyes had reached the level of the floor, the cockroach had disappeared from view, and there was nothing to be seen but a stretch of faded ingrain carpet.

She was too weary to continue the search, and so came back to the contemplation of the mantelpiece with its wooden dish of dusty exiles. Over the mantel hung an old engraving of a wooden-faced baby and a prim little girl with one foot under her, sewing. It was framed in black walnut, with a carved leaf at each corner, and the words "Watching Baby" were inscribed beneath. About the wall were its companions, framed in like manner. There was a chalk-faced woman with a low-necked dress and a sheet over the top of her head, gazing up into the sky with a sorrowful expression, called "Meditation." There also was that touching scene named "The Soldier's Farewell," where a stiff man and woman were clasped in each other's arms, with the various other stiff members of the family ranged about them. The girl turned from them in disgust, and with a curling lip which had in it more of weariness than of contempt, began to survey the rest of the room. The bedstead, bureau, and washstand were imitation cherry, and looked brisk and new, as if they could do cheap honors quite gracefully; but the fireplace had been covered with a thick coat of dull, black paint and looked discouraged, while the grate was one-sided, and imparted to the tongs and coal-scuttle a sort of down-in-the-mouth appearance. The table was a rickety old one belonging to another set, and covered with a moth-eaten red cloth with dirty cretonne storks sewed on by way of decoration. There was a cheese box covered with a dark green felt in front of the window, and that was all besides the two chairs and the occupant. There was a sort of despair in her face as she finished the inventory. The room was cheap, and had a good-sized clothes-press, and that was all that could be said in its favor. She tried to remember how much better this was than many a room which she had looked at, and to be thankful for having found this; but visions of a dainty white room furnished luxuriously, with all her precious belongings scattered about it, would come and imprudently contrast themselves with her present surroundings. How would her handsome jewel case look standing on that miserable stork table-cloth? But then she remembered that the elegant thing had been sold with everything else, and that there would be no need for it to associate with low-bred storks. Tears filled her eyes, and she went to the small-paned window to find some other occupation for her thoughts; but there came a knock at the door, and the announcement: "Your trunk has come, Miss; and the man asks, Where will he put it?"

When the trunk was unstrapped, and the man paid and gone, she went back to the window again. The street was quite dark now, and lights glinted about everywhere. She could see the tops of the heads of people as they passed the street lamp in front of the house. The hum and buzz of the wicked, busy city sent a shiver over her. It seemed a hundred times more terrible to hear it through the dark. She went back over her dreadful experience of the past few weeks. It did not seem possible that it had all happened to her, and she did not feel as if she could bear it. Perhaps it was a dreadful dream, and she would wake up tomorrow morning and find it past, and herself back in her own pretty room, with the door open into her mother's, and all her bright hopes hers again. But such could never be, and she must go on and bear her sorrow always. She turned and went in search of the slouchy Irish girl, to petition for a lamp, as there seemed to be no gas in the room.

Her story was like many she had read; but she had thought it could not happen to her — the sudden death of her mother, and shortly after that of her father; then the discovery that the money, which they had thought almost unlimited, was swept away, and that even the home must be given up. A familiar story, yet new and terrible to each one who passes through it. When she found that she must do something to earn her own living, she would have none of the ways that other girls in her position and with her accomplishments would have chosen.

"No," she said to a friend who tried to reason with her; "I can't do any of those things well enough, and I don't like to do them. Besides, places of that sort are full to overflowing already. If I knew how to cook

I would find a place as housekeeper some-where; but I don't. I can't do anything *well* but trim hats and bonnets!"

And trim hats and bonnets she would, despite all that could be said. She had done it for herself and her friends for years, and had always been said to have good taste. No one could place a feather or a bit of lace more gracefully.

Neither would she stay among her acquaintances and do her work; for she had found that in the general loss of home and money she had lost also some friends who had been counted as her very nearest and dearest. There was a pain in her heart to be fought with, and she longed to get away from everything familiar, and so had come to this strange city, rented a small store on a not very pretentious street, and with a lit-tle money that was saved from the wreck she would buy a small stock, and try her hand at millinery. A "cheap milliner," she told herself; for of course she could not hope to get the patronage of wealthy peo-ple at first.

This was her first night in her new home. She had had a long, weary day of store and room hunting, and before her were much work and worry before she could feel that she was really started. Life looked very hard to her that night.

"I hope yez won't be troubled much wid the roaches," said the woman who presided over the lamps, as she handed her a dripping, leering one.

"I thought there must be some reason for the cheapness," thought the weary girl as she dragged herself and her wicked lamp up the two flights of stairs. She opened the door, and lo! they had come to meet her — a whole army of them, great and small! They vanished from her in all directions, like the rays of light from the sun. She stood still in amazed disgust. She did not even attempt to catch one of them. So many cockroaches were more than her drooping spirits felt able to face at once. They all disappeared mysteriously in a moment, and left her the room. She looked toward the closet door tremblingly. Who knew how many generations of these horrid, shiny things were hidden behind its grim boards? Would they, *could* they, come out and crawl over her when she was asleep? This thought was too much. She put the lamp on the rickety table, closed the door, threw herself on the not overclean bed, and cried. So a great roach found her when he ventured to thrust his nose out under the closet door toward morning, to see why the lamp burned so long; but he dared not call out his tribe that night.

It was a bright Sunday morning's sun that peeped in and woke her a few hours later. She went drearily to church because she could not bear to spend the morning alone in that room; but she sat in a very back seat, and let the minister's sermon float over her head, as if it were something that must be gone through with, while she entertained bitter thoughts. She was glad when the long service was ended.

The people in the dismal little boarding-house across the way where she took her meals were tiresome, and so different from those by whom she was usually surrounded! She rushed back to her room from dinner as soon as possible, refusing the invitation to remain in the parlor and sing with the other boarders, so haughtily, that Miss Bangs, who gave it, walked back to the piano with a face the color of her old rose dress. She slept some, and unpacked some, and thought a great deal; and at last the day was gone. It was a great relief to think that she could go to work in the morning.

She really enjoyed buying her stock, tiresome though it was. She went from one wholesale store to another, and would take nothing but what was pretty or tasteful, though many a clerk assured her that certain articles were "just the craze," and would sell better than those she had chosen. She preferred good taste even to having "the correct thing," and remained firm.

"If I'm going to make bonnets for poor Irish girls, I'll see if I can't elevate their tastes. I just *cannot* put such ugly things together." Thus she told herself as she passed by boxes and boxes of hideous green artificial roses and various nameless imitations of what never grew upon the earth. Cheap things she was obliged to buy, for her purse was limited, and besides, she expected to serve people who would require cheapness; but there were plenty of inexpensive things that were also pretty. And so she spent much time and nerve, and at last had her little store ready for work. Of but one extravagance had she been guilty. She had found in one store a spray of small, white, starry blossoms, set among their fine, fern-like leaves, the whole thing so delicate and unobtrusive, and yet so natural and in such perfect taste, that it seemed to rest her tired eyes, which had all day been filled with gaudy colors and hideous straw shapes. They were fine French flowers, and very expensive. Her conscience and her judgment both rose up in horror; but she firmly put them down, and said to the clerk, "I will take them." Neither would she listen to these aggrieved advisers when she reached her room and they again tried to reason with her.

"There's no telling but I may have some very aristocratic customer, and she will demand such flowers. Anyway, they will help me to do my work. It will be pleasant just to know that they are there. Those wall-eyed daisies that I felt obliged to buy won't be able to hurt my feelings so much if these dainty, lovely things are in front of them." Thus she spoke to her conscience and her judgment, and they gave up in despair.

At last she was established. A neat sign over the door said MILLINERY in large letters, and underneath, a little smaller, "Miss M. L. Hathaway." She disliked the sign. It sounded stiff and far away, as if it were someone else who was being talked about, and not herself, Marion Hathaway. But of course she did not want to put that name out in the street for everyone to see.

It was just in the beginning of the spring

season, and customers began to come in. The dainty hats and bonnets that Marion had trimmed and placed in the window attracted much attention, they were so tasteful and unique. The orders came in so fast that she found she could not do everything herself, and must have someone to wait upon customers. She put a little sign in the window, "Girl wanted"; and there followed a procession of girls of various kinds, not one of them satisfactory to the fastidious milliner. At last, growing desperate, she resolved to hire the next girl that came in, good, bad, or indifferent. It was not more than five minutes afterward when in walked Miss Maria Bates. She wore very big sleeves, arranged her hair in a yellow knob at the back of her head, with two little stiff curls sticking out in the center, and a frizzle of bangs in front, and chewed gum vigorously. Marion's heart sank when she saw her; but she remembered her resolve, and engaged her. She gave the new clerk careful instructions as to her duties, and Miss Bates smilingly chewed the while. Marion later wondered if she chewed gum all night, for she never seemed to stop in the daytime. The young milliner sat behind a calico curtain and trimmed, establishing her new apprentice behind the counter. Whenever a customer entered the store, she arose, laid her hands upon the counter, and chewing, awaited a word from the incomer. It was on that same first Sunday of Marion's stay in the strange city that the young minister of Bethany Mission proudly led up the aisle for the first time a woman who to him was the most beautiful woman in all the world. It was her first Sunday in this city, and he took great joy in having her there and escorting her to church. It was only his old mother. You wouldn't have thought her beautiful. Her face was wrinkled, her hair was thin, and her bonnet looked very odd indeed. But her son did not think so. He had been in the city for years himself, and had seen fashionable women by the score, but it never occurred to him that his mother's dress was not all that it should be. He had not noticed that it was unlike others; and if he had, he would have thought her dress belonged distinctively to *his mother*, and suited her.

To be sure, she knew better herself, even though she had spent most of her life in the country. She had sighed, perhaps, over the faded shawl and wrinkled bonnet strings that had done duty for many years, and wished, down in her secret heart, that she might have some new things with which to make her advent in the city. But she knew that it was impossible. Even the money for her ticket had been hard to spare, and the salary from that struggling mission church was small. All this she knew; but she was not well versed in the fashions, and did not know that besides being old and faded, her bonnet was of a shape which looked, even to the members of that rough mission, odd, to say the least. They were city heathen, and knew what the fashions were, whatever else they did not know. It was plain that they expected better things of the minister's mother.

The young man proudly seated his mother and went to the platform. He bent his head in prayer a moment, and there was a note in it of tenderest thankfulness that at last he had his dear mother with him. When he raised his head he glanced again at the sweet, peaceful face sitting down in front of him. There were no wrinkles nor faded bonnet strings there for him. He saw only the happy light in the eyes he loved so well, and it seemed to help him. But he heard a titter; low it was, but unmistakably a titter. Just back of his mother sat two young women. They were dressed in some bright figured stuff, with large hats covered with gaudy flowers, and they were looking through their thicket of frizzed bangs straight at the big old bonnet ahead of them, and nudging each other. The young minister saw it, and wondered what it was about. He looked at his mother's bonnet, and at her. The ugly titter had brought a frown to his brow; but a glance at his mother's peaceful face, looking up at him so proudly, cleared it away, and he turned to the service with a thankful heart.

But when the sermon was ended and the last hymn was being sung, a shadow began to steal over his heart, and he wondered what was its cause. Some unpleasant memory seemed to be stirring. He glanced about the church, and his eye lighted upon those two girls again. Ah! he knew now what it was! A foolish thing, indeed, and not worth troubling over; and yet there lingered a disappointment in his heart that his mother had not inspired in others the admiration he always felt for her. How could one look at that dear beautiful face and laugh?

These reflections tinged the benediction with a little severity. He looked his mother over critically on the way home, all the time trying to decide what it was that the girls had been laughing at. As they met and passed two or three women, he saw them smiling and looking at his mother, and he heard one say in a loud whisper, "Just look at that ridiculous bonnet!"

Then he studied that bonnet! He compared it with all the bonnets he passed, and he began to realize that there was some difference.

"John MacFarlane!" said his mother as they neared the dingy house which contained the small rooms they called home, "that was a good sermon. You preach like your father, my dear. The blessing of the Lord be upon your work!" The mother beamed proudly up at her tall son.

And his happy heart forgot her bonnet for a little.

Chapter Two

It was a pleasant Sunday that this mother and son spent together. She had just arrived a day or two before, and there had been no time until now for one of those long talks that made his boyhood a tender and beautiful memory. There were old friends to be asked after in the country home, and many questions to be answered about his new parish work. Then they read a chapter in the Bible together as they had always done when he was a boy. As the twilight drew on, the mother spoke of his sermon again, and told him much about his father, things of which she had never spoken to him before. John felt as if a benediction had fallen upon him, and he hastened to his evening service with renewed zeal. Nevertheless, as the working days of a new week dawned, he found his heart oppressed with that bonnet! It troubled him all through Monday, and he studied more ladies as they passed on the street. He haunted the windows of fashionable millinery establishments, and tried to find out with his untrained eye what was the matter with his mother's bonnet. He told her once that if she needed any new things she must let him know, and he would give her money; and she thanked him, and thought of her old faded shawl and old bonnet strings, and said she guessed she could get along without anything a while longer. She even went so far as to take out her bonnet after dinner, and smooth out the crumpled strings, and sigh a little; but she put it back shortly into the clean little box where it had lived a long time. Poor old thing! It had done its best. It had seen hard service, and really, in its day, was neat, and even pretty.

What would the dear lady have thought could she at that moment have seen her grave son standing before Madame LeFoy's aristocratic millinery establishment, and looking with a puzzled, troubled expression at a large black tulle hat, rolled up triumphantly at one side, and bearing aloft in its gauzy arms a wealth of marvelous pink roses and buds, their thorny stems hanging gracefully over the edge of the brim? How would his mother look in that thing? He wondered dimly how they kept those flowers so fresh. They certainly must be real ones. He turned to another smaller headdress. It was all of violets, set close together, and bordered with their rich dark leaves. There was nothing but a strap of purple velvet for strings, and he wondered how they tied it. He walked to the other window. There was a silver gray bonnet with a sparkling tinsel cord for border, and many twinkling spears of steel oats gleaming among the forest of waving gray plumes that towered aloft. Everything else was pink and blue and scarlet. He turned from the window in despair. None of them would do for his mother. Other windows he looked in, with similar results, until it grew near the Sunday, and he began to fear for his sermon. He threw himself into his work then, and tried to forget the fashions; but he had a nervous feeling every time he thought of having that bonnet go to church. It was not that he was ashamed of his mother! He would have hated himself for such a feeling. It was that he was so proud of her that he could not bear to have her appear in something that to other eyes would hide the loveliness of her dear face.

When the next Sunday came, Mrs. Mac-Farlane was kept at home from service by a heavy cold. John, coming home alone that noon, was startled to find that there was a sort of relief in the thought that he had not had to preach facing that bonnet. He called himself all sorts of names for caring so much about a bonnet; but still he knew that it was true, and he resolved that something should be done about it the first thing Monday morning. What it was, or how it was to be done, he would not think now. This was the Lord's Day, to which belonged no bonnets of any sort or description. And he put it out of his mind.

But Monday morning bright and early he had a consultation with himself. The result was that he resolved to buy a new bonnet himself, and present it to his mother, cost what it might. Some milliner could help him, surely; and he was certain he could tell what would *not* do, although he did not know just what *would.* He took from his wallet a slender roll of bank notes, selected a two-dollar bill, and laid it on the table. He looked at it earnestly a minute or two, and then after some hesitation opened the wallet again and took out another two-dollar bill, adding it to the first. There was no telling what a bonnet might cost. Yes, he could spare that if it was necessary, and he counted the few remaining bills. Then he started on his mission. No minister of the gospel was ever sent on one more perplexing.

He went into the first millinery establishment he came to, which proved to be Madame LeFoy's. A tall, smiling girl advanced toward him, and inquired what she could do for him. He was slightly bewildered. He had never been inside one of these places before, and the hats and bonnets swaying on the wire frames standing about the room seemed to be whirling around him in wild confusion. He felt as if in a moment he would be surrounded and wafted away somewhere in spite of himself.

But he looked into the cold, steel eyes above the smiling mouth, and said, quite as though he were accustomed to shopping of this sort, "Could you show me something suitable for an old lady?"

She led him to one of the glass cases nearby, and took from it bonnets of various sizes, shapes, and colors, until the young man felt as if she had captured the rainbow, and was offering it for sale in patches.

"Here is one, just the thing for an old lady. Does she wear blue?" And she held aloft on her hand a small plat of golden-brown straw, faced with delicate blue, and trimmed with rich brown ribbon, and dreamy aigrettes of the same tint of blue.

John looked at it a moment, and then said he did not think she did wear blue.

"Not wear blue? Ah! Then how would a dash of red do? It is being worn very much now by old ladies — dull reds, you know," and she produced a gorgeous arrangement of various shades of dull reds, which John thought was a very large "dash" indeed.

He scowled at it and looked up at the rows of other bonnets for relief; but they shone with scorn at him out of their brilliancy. He put his hands in his pockets and looked down at the red dash thoughtfully.

"Haven't you something — ah, something not quite so — so — bright?" he asked.

"Something more subdued? Oh, certainly! Though I assure you these dull reds are quite the correct thing just now. A great many old ladies are buying them. It gives a youthful look to the face, you know."

John raised his eyes to the ceiling and waited during this speech, until the more subdued bonnet should be forthcoming.

"How would she like black? Here is something sober, though it is quite stylish too."

Black sounded hopeful. He turned to see. His first impression was that it was a small coal-scuttle with something stuck atop; but, as it came nearer, it winked and blinked hatefully at him, in patterns, from every tiny speck of its small space. The things atop seemed almost demonic in their jumping and dancing, and wicked lights shot out unexpectedly from their perfect blackness. It dazzled his eyes. He did not like it; but what was to be done? How did women get out of millinery stores, anyway, when they were not suited with the wares? But then he remembered that he had come to buy a bonnet, and a bonnet he must have, whether it pleased him or not. A dim thought crossed his mind that this thing was worse than the one it was supposed to supplant; but he decided to vary the monotony by asking the price.

"Twenty-five dollars," said the woman, deftly twirling it about on her fingers, and admiring it through the fringes above her eyes, "and cheap at that. It's *real* cut jet, you know."

No, he didn't know; but it didn't matter. He was appalled.

He managed to keep his face passive, however, and, to the woman, seemed to be considering the bonnet.

"Haven't you something cheaper?" he murmured, half under his breath. He felt as if all those hats and bonnets were so many stylish ladies listening and ready to laugh.

At that moment the door mercifully opened, and the steely eyes of Madame LeFoy were turned in another direction. He blessed inwardly the woman with a green bonnet who entered.

"Bella!" called Madame, "come and show the gentleman those bonnets in the last case on the left-hand side!" and she moved toward the newcomer, with the jet bonnet, twinkling impishly, still in her hand.

Bella came slowly out from the maze of hats and bonnets with an air of "don't care" about her. She led him to the back of the room, opened some glass doors, and took out a bonnet, holding it on her hand, and listlessly gazing out of the opposite window at a pile of packing-boxes in the backyard. She half sat on the little shelf that ran along below the glass, and he stood looking doubtfully at the rusty specimen she had placed before him. It was black, with a heap of feathers, and a few of those impish, jumping, jet things for trimming.

"How much is that?"

He asked the question grimly. What did people do for bonnets, anyway?

The girl brought back her eyes from the boxes, and studied a ticket pinned to one of the strings.

"Seven dollars and a half," she drawled.

He looked at it in dismay, as much as to say, "If *you* cost that, how can I ever find one that I can buy?" The bonnet seemed to lift its feathers with importance at him, but he turned away.

"Is that the cheapest you have?"

"Mis' LeFoy!" called the girl with a nasal

twang, "have you got anything cheaper'n this black bonnet here?"

"What, the one with feathers and jet? No!" said Madame.

"It's the cheapest we have," echoed the girl without moving from her seat on the shelf; but she raised her eyes from the boxes and set them upon the young man. He turned and walked out of the store with as much dignity as he could command, feeling all the time that the hats and bonnets were jeering at him. What should he do? He could breathe better now that he was out of the place, and he felt thankful for that; but he was no nearer the desired bonnet, apparently, than he had been a week before.

He paused before several other windows on Fourth Street, and then went on. The ribbons and feathers all seemed to be laughing at him, and he could not bring himself to go into those places. He walked on, scarcely knowing where he went, turning any corner he came to, until he halted before Marion's modest store. It was quieter here, and he could look into the windows without feeling that the passers-by were watching him. These hats did not look so flaunting and foolish as those at Madame LeFoy's. There was one small gray gauze hat on which nestled some tiny moss rosebuds. They looked like the buds that grew on the bush before the dear old farmhouse. He looked at them a moment, enjoying their perfect likeness. Then his eyes rested upon the white flowers which Marion had wrestled with her conscience and her judgment to buy. They were lying against some black net lace, and looked dainty and quiet. He felt immediately that they would fit his mother's face. So small and meek they looked amid their fine moss setting. The young man opened the door without more hesitation, and walked in.

Maria Bates arose with alacrity, and chewed with energy. A young man was at all times an interesting object to her. Young gentlemen customers were rare. This young man was very fine looking; and there was a dignified, high-toned bearing about him that penetrated even the brains under Maria Bates' yellow bangs. But then, her practiced eye noted the shiny look of the black coat he wore, and she decided that he was of no account. Therefore she placed her hands upon the counter, and waited for him to open the conversation. He seemed not anxious to do so, however. The moment his eyes rested upon the smart young curl at the end of the knob on the back of Maria's head, the restful assurance which the white flowers had brought him vanished, and he hardly knew where to begin.

He cleared his throat. It was apparent that the chewer on the other side of the counter did not intend to help him any. He took another step toward her, and cleared his throat again.

"I want to get" — and then he hesitated.

Miss Bates held her jaws midway, and waited for the rest of the sentence. He cleared his throat desperately, and began again, trying to make his voice sound natural.

"I want to get a bonnet!"

His voice sounded ghastly. He realized that he was in a trying position. But he said it, and surely he had a right to buy a bonnet if he paid for it. He looked at Maria in defiance. She slowly started her jaws again before asking, "For yourself?"

Marion, behind her shielding curtain, was sewing an obstinate feather in place and listening. Suddenly she drove her needle into her thumb, and with a jump which threw Sallie Hogan's new hat under the table, she stood up quickly.

"Maria!" she called in a very determined tone. Maria started, and stopped chewing for several seconds.

"Ma'am!" she answered meekly.

"I want you to take this ribbon up to Barnes & Brainard's, and match it immediately!"

"Can't just now! I've got a customer!" she answered.

"I will attend to the customer! I want the ribbon right away. Go, please, as fast as you can!" Marion said this decidedly, at the same time laying down her thimble and coming out from behind the curtain. Maria reluctantly took her jacket and hat from the nail in the corner, received her directions, and departed, still chewing.

Chapter Three

Marion turned to the young man, and asked, "Do you wish something trimmed or untrimmed?"

Ah! Here was a new question. How many there were connected with hats and bonnets! He knit his brows over it; and then as a picture floated before him of himself sitting at his study-table trying to trim a bonnet, his face broke into a smile.

"Trimmed, I guess," he answered. "I fear I shouldn't make much of a job at trimming it myself." Then he added more soberly, "I want to give it to her all ready to put on. It's for my mother. She's an old lady — not so very old, either, but she has white hair. I don't know what would be suitable. It seems to me that she would like something" — he hesitated, searching for the new word he had learned at Madame LeFoy's — "subdued," he added triumphantly.

There was no glitter of steel in Marion's eyes. They were brown, and, moreover, seemed to take in what he said, and appreciate it. She thought a moment.

"I do not think I have anything already trimmed that would suit," she answered, "but I think I could get up a bonnet that would please you. Would you like black or gray?"

He remembered the jet coal-scuttle, and was doubtful.

"I don't know, I'm sure!" he said desperately.

"Either would be quiet and suitable," she said; and, stooping to a box under the counter, she selected two bonnets of fine straw, one of gray and one of black. He took them, one in either hand, and looked at them. Was that the way they looked when the trimming was taken off? What remarkably innocent things they were, after all, he thought.

She could have laughed at the funny expression on his face; but she stood quietly waiting, and studying him. She began to wonder what the mother was like. There was something touching in this grave-looking young man buying a bonnet for his mother.

"How would you fix — how would you trim them?" he asked after a moment.

She took some ribbon and lace and a bit of velvet, and deftly laid them upon the bonnets. He was amazed to see what a difference it made in the hideous shapes.

"Then you might have some small flowers besides," she said.

"Flowers? Yes," he said, recollecting; "I saw some flowers in the window there that I liked very much," and he took two strides forward, and peered helplessly through the muslin curtain that separated the show window from the room. She drew the curtain aside, curious to see what was his taste in flowers. To her pleased surprise he pointed to the one rare spray of delicate blossoms. With a strange feeling she took them up, and placed them first upon one bonnet and then upon the other. He surveyed them with satisfaction.

"Yes; I like those," he said. "I think they would please Mother. They are like some flowers that used to grow in the garden at home."

"Which color do you prefer?" she asked.

"Which do you think would be most suitable?" he answered.

"How old is your mother?" she asked again, smiling. "If you would tell me how she looks I could judge better."

"She is about sixty. Her hair is white — but her face doesn't look old. She isn't very large — I never thought about exactly how she does look — but she has a very sweet, dear face," he answered tenderly, hesitating between the sentences, as if trying conscientiously to paint her portrait.

Marion was touched with his description.

"That's not old!" she said brightly. "I should think she would like the gray better. It is quiet enough for anyone. If she were very old I should choose the black, but for one only sixty I think the gray would be prettier."

He blessed her in his heart for saying that his mother was not old, and mentally compared her to Madame LeFoy. But those thoughts recalled another troublesome question.

"How much are such bonnets?" he suddenly said. "I find that they are much more expensive than I had supposed. Do you ever have anything as low as four dollars?" He tried to ask these questions in a dignified manner, but was conscious that it might be a most unheard-of thing he was asking. He would not have dared ask Madame LeFoy; but this milliner was quite a different being, and had taken an interest in his mother. He did not look up until she answered, but kept his eyes on the gray bonnet.

She was thinking. She took up a pencil, and fell to figuring, while John stood looking at the bonnets, and thinking how much better they looked than those on Fourth Street.

"If you had it without any flowers," said Marion at last, looking up, resting her elbow upon the counter and her head upon her hand, "I think I could make it for four dollars."

John was disappointed. He had not thought he could feel so disappointed about a bonnet. He glanced down at the little meek, starry blossoms, and they looked as if they felt sorry for him. Marion saw that he was disappointed, but he did not know it. He supposed that was a secret

216

between himself and the flowers, and he answered, "Very well. When can I get it?"

"I can have it ready by tomorrow morning, and you might come in any time after nine o'clock and see if it is what you wish. What is the name, please?" and she poised her pencil, ready to write it down.

"MacFarlane," he answered, bringing out one of the Bethany Mission invitation cards.

He breathed a deep sigh as he went out of the door. How tired he was! What a work it was to buy a bonnet! How did women stand it two or three times a year? And then, just as a woman would have done, he fell to worrying because he could not afford to buy the flowers. At the first corner he half turned to go back and ask their price; but his better sense reminded him that he could not afford another dollar, that it would positively take away from the necessary comforts which he hoped to give his mother, now that she had come to live with him, and he kept on toward home.

Marion watched him as he went out of the door, and then her eye came back to the bonnet and flowers. She somehow felt strangely sorry about those flowers. She picked them up, and laid them gracefully against the soft gray lace. They were pretty — very pretty. She figured a little more, shook her head, and then remembering that Barnes & Brainard's was not far away, and that Maria, with her inquisitive eyes, would soon be back, she took the white flowers and returned them to the window; but as she bent over to place them in just the right position, they seemed to look up wistfully at her. She studied her figures again, until she heard Maria's step outside, then hastily gathering up the gray bonnet and trimmings, she went to her workroom. But Sallie Hogan's green chip hat remained under the table, while she wrought out a sweet gray bonnet. She wondered to herself why it was that she took such pleasure in this special order, and tried to picture the face that would smile beneath the bonnet; and all the time the flowers troubled her, and she thought how much prettier and more perfect that bonnet would be with them on it. The young man's face, too, haunted her with its disappointed look. It was strange for a young man to care about flowers on a bonnet. He must have a good deal of taste himself, or he never would have noticed the difference. She glanced at his card that lay by her on the table, as she fashioned the gray ribbon into shining loops above the soft, white ruching border. Pastor of a mission chapel! His salary must be small, then! She could afford to be liberal to a poor young minister, and the flowers pleaded once more; but she told herself that she had already given much. She had promised to make the bonnet a great deal cheaper than she would have done for others, or than she could afford to do, either. She jerked her thread through and fastened it. It was her judgment and her conscience against her impulses once more. The gray bonnet was done; but its maker was not pleased with it, and placed it in a dark bandbox, dropping John MacFarlane's card after it, and shutting down the cover tight.

Then she brought out the green chip, and sewed fast. But white flowers hovered in her thoughts. She was disappointed in that gray bonnet. She took it out in the afternoon, and worked a whole hour upon it, and then tried it on, to persuade herself that it was better as it was; but all the time it seemed to lack something. It looked bare on one side. She put two more loops of ribbon in, but that seemed to do no good. After Maria had gone home that night she went to the window and took out the white flowers. She laid them on the bonnet in the vain hope that they would look too much, and take from, rather than add to, its beauty. But the sweet things seemed to nestle among the loops of ribbon as if they were meant for that place, and she fancied that they even smiled approval at her. She put them quickly back in the window, shut the bonnet in its box, turned out the lights, locked the door, and went home.

The faithful cockroaches met her at the door of her room as usual, escorted her in, and then vanished. It tired her already strained nerves to see them; but she was growing used to them. It had become a standing rule with her to shake every dress she took out of the closet until two had dropped out, and then she felt sure there were no more there. There were always two in each dress. She had tried everything to rid her room of them, but all had failed. She had made pills of borax and Indian meal, and daubed them all about, but they only seemed to thrive on that. She dusted everything with powder, and spread pieces of bread with ill-smelling compounds; but most of them remained unscathed, and only a few languid ones crawled out in search of water or medical assistance. She was very tired tonight, and it annoyed her exceedingly to know what a small thing had tired her. She sat down in the hard rocking chair; and conscience and judgment came and confronted her.

"We told you," they said, "that you ought not to buy those flowers. You knew that you could not afford them. You were weak — very weak. You bought them. When we upbraided you, you silenced us on the ground that some rich customer would want them, and now you want to *give* them away to someone you do not know at all, and all because a young man looked disappointed, and because a bonnet that you have made does not suit your extravagant taste!"

In vain did Marion bring up the picture of the mother, and her pleasure in the bonnet, and represent how much better the bonnet would look with those flowers. Judgment was inexorable. She gave up at last and went to bed.

She was in the little room back of the store early the next morning, trying once more to make the gray bonnet look as she thought it should. She was just holding it at arm's length, to discover what was the matter, when she heard the voice of her serving-maid. It was raised from the pleasant drawl she usually used in talking with customers, "Miss Hath'way, how much d'you say these little white flowers was?"

She lifted the curtain slightly, and peered out. There stood an elegant young lady with the flowers in one hand, waiting for her answer, while Maria was taking a leisurely survey of the customer's wardrobe, and getting pointers for her next shoddy suit. Marion made a sudden resolution, and dropped the curtain quickly.

"They are not for sale," she said quickly. "They are to go on a bonnet that goes out this morning."

Judgment stood appalled, while the young lady laid the flowers down in disgust, and walked out of the store.

"Now see what you have done!" said judgment. "You have lost a patron by that. She was a rich lady too. When you had a good chance to sell those miserable little flowers, you have thrown it away, and are going to *lose* the money you paid for them."

For answer she looked at the small clock on the table, and seeing it was almost the time she had set for the gray bonnet to be inspected, she sent Maria on an errand that was likely to keep her some time. She had no notion of having those eyes watching when the young minister came for the bonnet, nor of having her possibly overhear talk about the price. Maria well out of the way, she took the bonnet out once more, and went for the flowers. Her fingers trembled slightly as she fastened them, but she felt triumphant. Perhaps it was foolish, but it was nice. She was tired of having judgment lord it over her. She liked to follow her own sweet will once in a while, and it was nobody's business but her own what she did with those flowers. Since she had bought them against her judgment, why should she not dispose of them without consulting that autocrat? The knob of the store door was turned just as she fastened the last stitch. There was a glow of excitement in her eyes, and her cheeks were slightly flushed. She went out to wait upon the young minister in her store with the same grace which had made her charming in society.

Chapter Four

Before she opened the box she explained to him that she had found she was able to make the bonnet and put the flowers on for the price he had mentioned; and then she brought it forth. There was unmistakable delight in John MacFarlane's eyes as he viewed that bonnet. The soft white ruche looked to him just like his mother; and the dainty flowers, settled among the rich folds of gray ribbon, seemed like small Quakeresses. It was quietness itself, and yet he felt with pride that it could hold up its head with any aristocratic bonnet at Madame LeFoy's.

"I like it," he said simply. "I'm so glad for the flowers."

It seemed as if he were thanking her for a favor done as to a personal friend, not at all in a businesslike way.

She put the bonnet carefully in its wrappings in the box; and as she did so the flowers seemed to nod to her and say, "You have done right. You will not be sorry."

John, as he proudly paid for his bonnet, thanked her for the help she had given him. He felt almost as happy this morning as when he was a little boy and had a holiday in which to go fishing. That bonnet had troubled him all night, in dreams appearing in various forms, until he had come to fear that his mother never would be able to wear it. He had gone after it this morning very doubtfully. He wished he had never thought of a bonnet, and almost feared to go in and look at it; and, lo! here it was, flowers and all, and prettier than any bonnet he had seen for twenty-five dollars even. How could he help expressing some of his delight?

"I shall tell my mother that you helped about this, and she will be very grateful, I'm sure. I never could have found one if someone hadn't helped me, I'm afraid," he said as he was going out.

It was a strange thing to say to a milliner, perhaps, but he said it. She smiled, and said she was glad to have helped, and she hoped his mother would like the bonnet; and then he was gone, and she went back to her work.

It was lonely with the flowers gone. Perhaps it was foolish, after all, for her to have put them on; but she was glad she had done it, and she wished she could peep in at the window when the bonnet was presented, and see the mother, and hear what was said. She thought of her own mother, and tears gathered in her eyes. She brushed them away. The flowers had somehow started painful thoughts. By and by Maria came back, and chewed and waited on a few customers; and the day wore away until Marion could go back to her dreary little room and her cockroaches.

John MacFarlane carried his white box proudly through the streets. He felt already

225

that he could give a better heart to his next sermon. He looked in at Madame LeFoy's triumphantly as he passed. As he neared home he began to wonder just how he should present his gift, and wished it was Christmas, or that there was a birthday somewhere for an excuse. He began to feel awkward about it, and finally decided to put it away until Saturday evening, when he and his mother were having their after-tea talk. He had trouble getting it out of sight, and changed its hiding place often, lest his mother, in clearing up, should stumble upon it, and spoil his surprise. Then he waited for Saturday evening to arrive with as much impatience as a boy waits for Christmas morning. Two or three times he took the box out and lifted the tissue-paper wrappings to get a peep; and the flowers always smiled up reassuringly. Over his study, his work, and even his pastoral visits, during that week the gray bonnet hovered like a pleasant thought.

The hour came at last; and, her work all done for the week, his mother sat down by the bright student lamp with her knitting. Now was the time. He went to his study, and brought the box from its hiding place.

"Mother, I have a present for you," he tried to say calmly; but in spite of himself there would steal into his tone some of his old boyish eagerness.

"Why, bless you, boy! What have you there?" she said with pleasant inquisitiveness, looking over her glasses at the box, and holding her knitting with both hands.

He untied the cord, pulled aside the wrappings, drew out the bonnet, and held it awkwardly on his hand. There was triumph in his eyes, and pleased surprise in his mother's. Neither of them spoke for a full minute.

John stood with his head a little to one side, taking a back view of the bonnet, and seeing how it would appear to the two gigglers if they should come to church again tomorrow.

And the mother looked at it, and at her handsome son, and then away beyond the bonnet into her past. Tears gathered in her eyes.

"John, dear boy!" she said, and her voice trembled slightly, "your father did just that for me once. You're like your father, John."

The tender tones touched the young man's heart. It pleased him beyond anything to know that he was like his father. He went over to his mother, bent, and kissed her forehead. She put out her hand for the bonnet, and held it off admiringly, then drew it nearer, and smoothed lovingly the shining folds of rich new ribbon. She liked bonnet strings that were not crumpled.

"It's a beautiful bonnet, John. I'm afraid you've been extravagant. I'm nothing but an old woman now, you know, and anything would do for me." But she looked with pleased eyes upon the flowers.

"The dear things!" she said. "They look so like the little flowers that bloomed in our front yard at home. You don't remember them, I suppose. It seems as if I must smell them," and she bent her head toward them.

John still stood by her, watching, well-satisfied, pleased as any boy at the praise she gave it.

"Mother, tell me about the other bonnet, the one father brought you?" he said with a gentle, questioning intonation.

The tears came to her eyes again, and that faraway, longing look settled over her face.

"It was before we were married, dear," she said. "He had heard me say that I must have a new bonnet; and so one day when he went to the city he remembered it, and brought me one when he came back."

She smiled to herself as she said it, looking off in the shadowy corner of the room. She could almost see her tall young lover standing with the bonnet in his hand, and waiting for her admiration, even as her son had just stood. How it all came back to her — the pleasure they had in trying it on, and the walk in the moonlight afterward! It seemed but a few days ago; and now here was her son, as old as his father had been, and doing the same thing, only the bonnet was not so youthful as the other had been.

"It was a white bonnet, John!" she said, turning back to his face lovingly. "You think your old mother would look odd in a white bonnet now, don't you? Well, so she would, but she looked nice in it then. It was white straw, trimmed with white ribbon, and tied with white strings, and it had a soft white ruching inside, just like this one," she said, touching the lace tenderly, "with a fine, green vine mixed in with it!"

They talked some time about that other bonnet; but by and by came back to the present, and admired the new one again.

"I never should have known what to get, if it hadn't been for that young lady."

"What young lady?" asked his mother with keen interest. Her son had up to now, in her judgment, been almost too indifferent to all womankind except herself.

"Oh, I suppose she was the milliner, though she did not seem like one in the least. Try it on, Mother, and let's see if it is becoming."

Mrs. MacFarlane nervously smoothed down her shining, unrumpled white hair, and taking hold of the bonnet just where the strings were fastened on, raised it to her head, settled it, and looked at her son, still holding the strings with one hand under her chin.

"Why, Mother! It makes you look younger, I declare!" he said. "She said sixty wasn't old. Don't let me hear you calling yourself an old woman. You won't be an old woman these ten years yet. It actually takes some of the tired look out of your eyes. You're the prettiest woman I know of, Mother!" he said, kissing her again. He brought a faint pink to her wrinkled cheek. She looked at her son proudly, as she raised her face to return the kiss.

"You're like your father, John," she said again.

Then there was more talk about the bonnet and the milliner; and Mrs. MacFarlane said she would like to see her and thank her.

That same evening Marion was sitting in

her dreary little room, thinking. She was too weary to read or work, and so she sat listlessly, letting her idle thoughts wander where they would. They settled presently upon the gray bonnet and white flowers. She wondered where they were tonight, and if they would go to church tomorrow. Suddenly a strange fancy seized her. She would go to that little mission chapel, and see what sort of a face would appear under the bonnet. She would like to see the flowers doing their appointed work in the world, and know if they fitted their surroundings; and whether, after all, judgment had been right, and she wrong. The new fancy pleased her. It would perhaps be interesting, to see what sort of a sermon that young man would preach. At any rate, it would do no harm, and she meant to go and try it. It would relieve the monotony of the day, and serve to keep the painful thoughts away.

And so it came about that the next morning when John MacFarlane proudly escorted the gray bonnet down the aisle, and seated it in front of the two gaudy gigglers, the maker of the bonnet sat in a back seat and watched them.

She could not catch a glimpse of the face beneath its soft gray framing; but she noticed with relief that the bonnet was set upon the head as it should be, and that the bearing of the woman who wore it was dignified and refined, although her black shawl was a trifle threadbare. The instant she saw it she thought of the beautiful India shawl which had belonged to her mother, and was now packed away in one of her unused trunks. But that was only a passing thought. She turned her eyes to the young man, and noted the pride with which he seated his mother. His face was very grave, and without the slightest tinge of conceit.

She examined the audience critically. They were of all sorts. A few well-to-do; many of them poorly dressed. Some of the children were even ragged. It was the strangest audience she had ever seen gathered in a church. She watched the young minister during the opening exercises, and tried to remember that this grave, dignified man, who seemed to feel so thoroughly at home in the pulpit, was the same one who had been ill at ease, and almost embarrassed, over a bonnet a few days before.

"Their Redeemer is strong; The Lord of hosts is his name: he shall thoroughly plead their cause, that he may give rest to the land, and disquiet the inhabitants of

Babylon." That was the text. Marion listened carefully. The words sounded new to her; she did not remember to have ever read them. She watched the faces of some of the children as the preacher described the Redeemer, and fastened the explanation to their wandering minds by telling a simple story. She was interested in the story herself. It was restful to think of something strong. She was tired and lonely, and felt as if she were a captive in a strange land. This was simple preaching. Marion, as she listened, realized as she had never done before, what it would be to have the Lord of hosts for her Redeemer. What rest it would bring to her heart to know that he was pleading her cause! The young minister's hearers could but ask themselves, "Am *I* in the captivity of sin, as those people were captives in Babylon? Is the Lord of hosts *my* Redeemer? Can *I* rest in the belief that he is pleading *my* cause?"

Chapter Five

Marion was surprised when the sermon was over. It had seemed but a few moments. As she bent her head for the closing prayer, the first words of the text kept ringing in her ears: "Their Redeemer is strong."

She had unconsciously expected to find many things to criticize in this young minister, but as she thought it over during the closing hymn, she found she could remember scarcely anything that he had said. She only knew that she had felt all through her heart what Jesus Christ wanted to do for her if she would let him. He seemed a real person to her. She felt the presence of the great invisible army of the Lord of hosts all about her.

During the general rush that followed the benediction, Marion stood still at her seat to let others by, and avoid getting into the press. She turned, hoping to get a glimpse of the face under that bonnet; for, after all, that had been her object in coming. The white flowers seemed to smile a pleasant greeting to her across the heads of the moving people. The minister came quickly down from the pulpit, leaned across two seats, and whispered a word to his mother; and then they came toward her. She did not realize that they were coming to speak to her until they were very near. Her eyes were upon the peaceful face of the minister's mother. She noted that the bonnet was becoming, and that it fitted exactly the kind of woman she was; and then she forgot to look at the bonnet in her admiration of the perfect happiness of the face beneath.

John MacFarlane stood before her, bowing respectfully.

"My mother has wanted to see you very much," he said, and turned toward the gray bonnet at his shoulder.

Mrs. MacFarlane took both of Marion's hands in her own, and said in her hearty, motherly tone, "I have wanted to see you, dear, and thank you for the help you gave my son. He has told me all about it, and I thought I'd like to tell you that I like it very much."

It was so sweet to Marion to be called "dear" once more by someone, that she utterly lost all her milliner's dignity, and answered with a little of her old girlishness, that she was so glad Mrs. MacFarlane liked it; and she glanced up again at those flowers, that actually seemed to be almost winking at her, modest little Quakeresses though they were, and in a church at that. And then they went out together into the pleasant spring sunshine.

"Oh, isn't this a beautiful Sunday? God must take delight in making such days for us!" said Mrs. MacFarlane as they came down the steps. "You must be very glad, dear, when this day comes, and you can get away for a little while from your store."

Marion's face clouded over.

"Sunday is a dreary day for me," she answered. "I am alone in the city. There isn't anything pleasant about a boarding-house Sunday, Mrs. MacFarlane!" Then she suddenly realized that she was not this woman's friend, as she had almost felt a moment before, only her milliner.

"All alone!" said the sympathetic voice. "But God is here. You can enjoy him! A boarding-house must be a dreary place, though. Is your home far from here?"

"I have no home now," said Marion sadly. "My father and mother are gone, and I am the only one left. I am trying to make this my home; but it is hard work," and she smiled a pitiful little flicker of a smile at the kind face bent toward her.

"Now, dear child, is that so? It must be very lonely for you then, truly. I know what it is to have dear ones leave me; but I never was left entirely alone," and she looked up at her tall son with loving pride.

"I'll tell you what you shall do," she said suddenly, turning back to Marion. "You shall come home with us to dinner. We've nothing very nice, to be sure; but I'd like to have you, and let me play you are at home for a little while. I'll try to cheer you up a bit. We haven't known each other very long, but I think we could be friends. The King's children ought always to be able to get acquainted quickly."

Marion paused at the corner where she turned off toward her boarding-house, and looked down, hesitating, and somewhat embarrassed. A great desire had seized her to accept this invitation. She had been on the point of declining politely; but, glancing at the motherly face, she wavered. She longed to be inside a real home once more.

"Do come!" said the minister. "We would be very glad to have you."

And so, after a little demurring, instead of declining, she turned and walked on with her new friends, horrified judgment berating her all the while.

They talked of the beautiful day, and various other trifling matters of which people speak when they are just feeling their way into an acquaintance with one another. After her first surprise at finding herself in this strange and unexpected situation, Marion began to enjoy it. It was so pleasant to have some friends to talk with once more. They came presently to the

sleepy-looking house where the Mac-
Farlanes lived. It was not one whit less
dreary looking than the one in which
Marion had her room; but there were
white curtains at the windows, which gave
such a feeling of hominess, that it seemed
to her a palace in comparison.

Seated in the little parlor alone a few
minutes later, with the soft spring wind
blowing in at the open window, swaying
the ruffles on the dimity curtains, and fan-
ning her cheeks, she was obliged to admit
to herself that she had done a very strange
thing, to say the least, in accepting this invitation. Nevertheless, she was unable to
feel at all sorry about it. This room was so
cozy and homelike, with its plain furnish-
ing, and air of happy, neat contentment!
Mrs. MacFarlane had emerged from her
bedroom a few moments before, her black
dress enveloped in a large clean apron; and
while she pinned it around her ample
waist, told Marion to rest, and make herself at home for a few minutes. Then she
had gone to the kitchen, and her son had
followed her. She could hear their voices
now through the unlatched door. By the
sound, she judged that the young man was
bringing wood, making a fire, and then
drawing water, and helping his mother

about little things. She shut her eyes, and let the breeze cool her lids. It was so pleasant.

Presently the minister came back. The talk drifted upon books; and she found that they had read many in common. It was a treat to her, this being able to speak of favorite books again with someone who knew them and loved them.

Marion, as she sat down to the small white table, wondered when she had ever been so hungry. There was not so great a variety for dinner, nothing so elaborate as they would have had at her boarding-house; but everything looked nice. The cold meat, cut into thin, pink slices, and the warmed-up potatoes, had a homelike taste. Homemade bread, too, was a rare treat to her now, and the coffee was just right. She asked about the Mission Chapel and its work, and gained a new idea of city missions. After dinner she would help with the clearing away, though Mrs. MacFarlane said that she could do it alone, and that Marion was to rest. But she persisted, and then they talked. Marion found that the mother was fully as intelligent as the son. But it was after the work was done, and they came back to the little parlor to sit down and talk, that there came the most helpful time for Marion. It was a talk that she remembered all her life afterward with thankfulness.

The minister had gone to his mission chapel, and they were alone. His mother had coaxed from Marion, little by little, the story of her sorrows; and she had told it with trembling lips. The elder woman had listened sympathetically to it all.

"But, Mrs. MacFarlane," Marion said, looking up as she finished the recital, "you are mistaken in me about one thing. I do not want to wear a false character. You said I was one of the children of the King, and I'm not."

Her head drooped low over the last words, and the tears gathered in her eyes while she waited for a reply. It came in a loving, but sorrowful and disappointed tone.

"Not one of the children of the King, dear? Whose child are you, then?"

"Whose am I?" asked Marion, startled and puzzled.

"Yes, dear," said the voice, so tender and sad. "You must belong to someone. Whose child are you, if you aren't the King's?"

"Oh, don't!" said the girl, shuddering, and hiding her face in her hands. "That is dreadful! I never thought of it so before."

Then she felt a loving arm around her. "Dear child," said the sweet voice again, "you are one of the King's children, even though you have not been serving him. Don't you know he bought you with a price? You are his, only you have been serving someone else, and have not acknowledged your true Father."

It was a long talk they had. Marion's tears flowed fast at first, but gradually she began to see the light. She knelt with Mrs. MacFarlane, and gave herself to Christ, and arose with a new feeling of peace in her heart. Her soul had been reaching out for help for a long time, but she did not know where to go to satisfy the great longings which had filled her. Now she felt that Jesus Christ was going to fill her heart, and that all would be different.

The afternoon went swiftly by, and she had hardly realized that time was passing until she suddenly remembered that it was growing dark, and that the walk home was not a short one. She hastened away, then, but not until they had made her promise to come again.

Chapter Six

She thought it all over when she sat alone in her little room that evening. How strange it had been — the bonnet, the flowers, her resolve to go to the chapel, the invitation, and now the wonderful Presence that seemed to fill her heart and overflow into the room! She glanced about. She did not seem to mind the dusty shells with their mockery of the sea, nor the forlorn engravings, nor even the cockroaches. She had something now to be really happy over; and she hummed a little tune as she went about her preparations for rest.

A determination was forming itself in her mind, and it grew stronger as the week progressed. She would go to that little chapel every Sunday. To be sure, it was quite a walk; but what was that? It would do her good. Besides, her only friends in the city were there, and she had found more good there than in any of the other churches she had attended. To be sure, she had not been in the right frame of mind to get good from the other churches; this she realized: but she had a longing after the chapel, and she meant to go. She began to decide that her judgment would have to be reeducated.

It was not long before her new pastor called upon her, and then called again, and brought his mother, who took her in her arms and kissed her, and called her, "My dear," quite as if she were an old friend. It brought a warm glow to Marion's lonely heart to feel that she had such friends, and life looked less dreary to her after that call.

It was only the following Wednesday evening that she was sent for to come down to the dingy parlor of her boarding-house; and there stood Mr. MacFarlane, hat in hand. Would she like to go to the chapel prayer meeting? If so, he would be pleased to have her company. It was so pleasant a walk, and the young minister was so entertaining, that it thoroughly rested her after her day's confining work. Then the prayer meeting was so homelike, and helped her as she had not been helped in many a year. She found herself wondering why she had never been to prayer meetings before. After that John MacFarlane frequently stopped for her on his way to meeting; and it made a bright spot in the midst of the long, busy week for the little milliner.

One afternoon John stepped into the store to bring a note from his mother, begging that Marion would take tea with them that evening. On this occasion Maria was out, and he looked about him at the bonnets, and wondered that he had ever been so afraid of one. He felt himself a connoisseur in bonnets now.

Marion had many pleasant times in the small, cheery parlor of the MacFarlanes. There was a restfulness and peace which she had never found in any of the homes of her fashionable friends. The young minister dropped into the store often to bring these delightful invitations. Now and then he brought a book which he thought would please her. Once or twice he asked her company to a fine lecture or concert; and so, little by little, they grew to be better acquainted.

The busy summer flew by more pleasantly than Marion had imagined it could, and the autumn came on. When the wind began to blow chilling messages from the approaching winter, Marion thought of her mother's shawl, and she looked for several Sundays meditatively at the rather thin black one that Mrs. MacFarlane wore to church. She unpacked hers one day from its camphor wrappings, and shook it out in soft folds upon her bed. Then she sat for a long time with tears in her eyes. Would she, could she, give it up — her mother's shawl? She did not expect to use it herself, it was true. It would hardly be suitable for her. Besides, she had other warm wraps, and did not need it. But would Mrs. MacFarlane accept it? Could she bear to give up the shawl, and see someone else wearing it, when it reminded her so of her dear mother?

"But Mother would be pleased if she knew it. She always gave her beautiful things away. I know she would like it. And Mrs. MacFarlane has been so good to me, and I love her very much," she said to herself.

A few days thereafter the shawl, wrapped in heavy paper, and bearing Mrs. MacFarlane's address, was sent to her by a small brother of Maria Bates, who happened to be playing marbles outside the store. There was a little note accompanying it which touched the dear lady even more than the gift of the shawl had pleased her, which was saying a good deal. She read it through twice, and then with tears in her eyes she said, "Dear child!" and, wiping the moisture from her glasses with the corner of her smooth, white handkerchief, she handed it over to her son:

Dear Mrs. MacFarlane,

You have been so very good to me, and I love you so much, that I want to send you this shawl. It was my dear mother's, and I would like to see you wearing it. I think, too, it would please her. She must love you for having brightened the lonely life of her child. Please accept it as a slight token of the gratitude and love I have for one who has helped to bring peace to my heart.

> Yours lovingly,
> Marion Hathaway

The shawl was a welcome surprise to Mrs. MacFarlane. She had just been planning to make her thin black one do all winter by folding a smaller thick red one inside it; but even then it would have been thin. Her son was more pleased than he expressed even to his mother. He enjoyed seeing her with the heavy, beautiful shawl around her. It always seemed to him that beautiful things belonged to his mother, though she looked queenly to him in the commonest thing she wore.

It was toward spring again, almost a year from the time when Marion and Mrs. MacFarlane had first come to the city. The postman rang at the MacFarlanes', and handed John, who came to the door, a letter. He glanced at the postmark in feverish haste, then went to his study, and closed the door behind him, tearing open the letter as if it contained some important message. As he read, the anxious, wistful look on his face changed to one of gladness. He half turned to open the door and read it to his mother; but, thinking better of it, reached up to the hook behind his study door for his hat and overcoat.

"I'm going out for a little while, Mother," he said as he passed through the sitting room.

He went with rapid steps down the street, never looking up at the bright-eyed spring bonnets that nodded to him from Madame LeFoy's window. On he went, straight to the little side street where lived his milliner.

"May I come into your work room for a few minutes?" he asked Marion, as she came forward, smiling, to meet him. "I want to talk a little, and I don't want to hinder you. Maria is safe," he said reassuringly, as he saw Marion hesitate, and glance uneasily out of the window. "She has reached only the next corner above here with the bonnet you have sent her home with, and she is talking with a young man. She's likely to stand there some time yet, I should say. How far had she to go?"

"Away over to East Fletcher Street," Marion answered happily. "Come in. I wouldn't let you, only I'm very busy this morning."

He sat down; she took up her work, and they talked pleasant commonplaces for a minute or two, when he said suddenly, "I have received a call to Springdale!" and handed her the letter which had come that morning.

She started slightly, but took the letter, and read it. The color mounted into her face; but her lips wore their firm little curve, with perhaps more dignity than usual.

"It is a very good salary, and a pleasant field for work, I should think," she said, trying to speak composedly; "but I —" she hesitated, and a flush mounted up into her face. She began again "We shall —" she caught herself once more, the red in her cheeks spreading even to her forehead. She realized that there was no one, unless it were Maria Bates, in connection with whom she might use that pronoun "we."

She resolved this time to gain entire control of herself, and, straightening up a refractory loop of ribbon, began the sentence once more. "Your congregation will miss you very much indeed," she said, this time in a clear, unnatural voice; and then realizing that she had made a decided muddle of things, and feeling vexed over it, she thrust her needle through ribbon and bonnet and finger with a force which set every nerve tingling in sympathy with the poor abused finger. When she looked up it was only to find the minister's eyes full upon her, and an amused expression on his face.

"Finish your first sentence, won't you, please?" he asked in a tone that demanded an answer.

She looked down a moment.

"It began with 'I,' " he said, as she still hesitated.

"I shall miss your mother very much indeed," she finished quickly, with a demure air, and went on with her work, though her cheeks were glowing.

Then they both laughed. He recovered his gravity first. Perhaps he realized that Maria Bates' continued absence was uncertain, and his time might be short. He put the letter in his pocket, and drew his chair close to hers.

"Marion," he said, taking both her trembling, cold hands into one of his, and with the other landing the bonnet she was sewing, with all its trimmings, right into the middle of a box of crush roses, "will you go to Springdale with me, and help me begin the new work?"

If Maria Bates had but known what was going on behind the calico curtain in the little store that morning, she would not have stood smiling and simpering so long on the corner of Second Street with the young man who wore so elegant a paste-diamond scarf-pin. But the world moves on, and waits for none. Even Maria Bates and young Mosely were called, by what they used for a conscience, to move on; and in course of time Maria had finished her errand, and was on the way back.

Marion finally succeeded in impressing this fact upon John MacFarlane; and he discreetly took himself away, just in time to escape Maria's scrutinizing glance, promising, however, to return at six o'clock precisely that evening and take her home to his mother.

"Mother," he said a little after six, as he threw open the parlor door, and stood so that he filled the doorway entirely, "I have a present for you."

"Bless the boy! What is it? Another bonnet?" she asked mischievously, looking at him with a twinkle in her eyes.

"No, it's not a bonnet this time; it's the milliner herself." And he stood aside triumphantly, and gently pushed the blushing Marion in front of him.

Now the cockroaches are looking for a lodger, and the store windows where once smiled the white blossoms are full of candy canes and dogs and cats, with a box of cigars and a few wilted bananas by way of variety; and many ladies who were just beginning to find out Marion's dainty taste are wondering what has become of that elegant little milliner who made such "loves of hats at such ridiculous prices!"

But there is a small white parsonage with green blinds, set in the midst of a wide green lawn which slopes away on the right to a pretty stone church, somewhere. On the porch in pleasant weather sits a lovely old lady, whose hair is crowned by beautiful soft white caps. She knows what has become of the milliner, and so does the minister. And the people who live in the pleasant village streets, and out on the green hills nearby, love her with all their hearts.

"Living Epistles"

Tom Rushmore was seated in the evening train, tapping his toe impatiently as he waited for the signal to start. He had been detained until this 6:30 train; and he was in a hurry to be home, for there was dinner to be eaten, and several little things to attend to before evening service. He did not really see how he could spare the time to go to the meeting that evening, but he had promised that earnest-faced sister of the new minister that he would come. He was sorry now that he had done it. It was never wise to make promises; but now that he had given his word he must keep it.

Just then, with a burst of rather hilarious laughter, there entered a group of young girls with books under their arms. They seemed to be bent on some sort of lark; for their spirits were out of all keeping with the amount of amusement on hand, so young Rushmore thought. He turned to look out of the window, thinking no more about them. But here came *more* young people with the same kind of books under their arms, and behind them one or two older gentlemen and two ladies, who seemed to belong to the same group!

He looked curiously at the book in the hand of a young man that stood talking just under his window. *"Gospel Hymns No. 6, Christian Endeavor Edition,"* he read. It struck him as rather curious that a company of young people should be boarding the train on a week night, with copies of religious singing books under their arms. Then he remembered that this must be the delegation of Christian Endeavorers that was coming out to Brinton to hold that wonderful meeting that he had promised to attend. Now he would have a chance to study them beforehand, and see whether they were as extraordinary people as he had been led to suppose.

A bevy of young people were on the back platform just behind him. There was a great deal of loud laughter, and some of them seemed to be uproarious. All at once, with an explosion of merriment, a young girl was pushed into the car. She was nicely, stylishly dressed, and had a pretty, refined face, which was hardly in keeping with her actions.

She stumbled up the aisle of the car,

calling aloud to her friends: "Come on, Mamie! Let's get the best seats! Here, Charlie, here's a place! Hurry! Quick! before Fred gets here; he'll take everything there is going! Here, Jennie, give me that peanut-bag. You selfish thing! You aren't going to eat them all up, are you?"

The party had turned over a seat opposite Tom Rushmore; so he had opportunity to watch all that went on without being observed. Indeed, the entire car was treated to their conversation, whether they would or not, the tones were so loud. The young girl that had first come, or rather been pushed, into the car, and who he found was addressed as Fanny, seemed to be a sort of leader among them, though the others very readily followed, and some went farther than she after she had started. She had beautiful teeth, and showed the entire set whenever she laughed, which was nearly all the time. Just as the train started, several belated ones entered the other end of the car.

"Oh, there comes Will at last!" said Miss Fanny, rising in her seat, and waving her handkerchief violently. "I was afraid they'd get left; his sister is always late. Will, come down here! You can sit on the arm of Charlie's seat," she called from one end of the car to the other, in a voice that would have been very sweet if it had not been at so high a pitch, and so loud.

Almost every one in the car but the young man addressed looked around to the young woman that was making so much demonstration; but he was looking for a seat, and neither saw nor heard her, strange to say. She was not to be thus balked in her purpose, with all those people looking at her too. She was not a bold girl, only young and thoughtless; but she walked — or maybe "pranced" would be a better word — up that aisle, took possession of the young man, and escorted him to their "crowd," as she phrased it.

Then the train started; and the merriment, and peanuts and taffy with which they had provided themselves without stint, ran high. Some very slangy jokes reached the ears of the young man across the aisle, and he curled his lip as he remembered the words of the earnest-faced young woman that he had heard that morning: "They are very fine young people that have taken hold of this Christian Endeavor movement, Mr. Rushmore, and you ought to be numbered among them. Even if you do not feel that you can call yourself a Christian, you might become an associate member. I am sure you would enjoy the social part of it. And I am sure you cannot be with them long without seeing how much like Jesus Christ some of them are, and without learning to want him for your own friend."

Tom Rushmore liked the minister's sister; for one thing, because she always spoke out plainly what she had in her mind, instead of trying to honey-coat everything, and wheedle you into going somewhere for some other reason than the real one. He liked to have her say just that to him, to make him feel that, while he might enjoy the social part of these meetings, still, that was not the real object of her asking him to come, after all. It had been that feature of her request that had caused him to promise, even against his inclination, to go to that meeting. He had a feeling that she had been fair and square with him, and that to be the same with her he would either have to do as she wished, or say plainly, "I don't want to have anything to do with this society, and I don't want to learn to love Jesus." This he did not think it was exactly courteous to say. But he thought of it now, and felt sorry for her, as some sad, wise man might feel sorry for a poor deluded angel that had lost her way. These Christian Endeavorers were not what she thought them, after all. Well, it was just as he had supposed.

Just at this point in his meditations the train slowed up at a station, and the words became distinctly audible again.

The young man called Will was addressing Miss Fanny.

"Say, Fanny! I think you are a pretty hilarious crowd to be going to a religious meeting, aren't you?"

The young girl flushed prettily, and said, "Did you suppose we had to be long-faced just because we belonged to the Christian Endeavor Society? No, indeed! We believe in having a good time, don't we, Mame?"

Then they all giggled.

"Have some more taffy, Will. It's good, isn't it?" went on Fanny. "This is a regular picnic, you know; and we don't have to act as we do at home. It isn't Sunday, either."

"What are you going to do tonight?" asked the young man again, who seemed to wear no badge, and had no singing book.

"Do?" queried Fanny brightly. "We're going down to convert those Brinton people. We're missionaries, don't you know? I think it's just delightful. They say these meetings do ever so much good. Lots of new members will join just on account of our coming out there tonight. Just wait till you've been to the meeting."

"I know one that won't join," murmured Tom Rushmore under his breath, with haughty scorn in his face, as he prepared to leave the train. "However, I've promised to go, and I suppose it will disappoint Miss Bowman if I don't; but they've spoiled the meeting for me. Maybe it isn't fair to judge them all by one or two, though there were a good many of them that were rather ill-behaved; but perhaps they were the associate ones, and haven't got converted yet themselves. I'll go and see."

The merry party trooped down the shaded street of Brinton toward the pretty church situated in a grove of maples, while the young man that had been watching them went on his way home.

"They have grand societies in the city," Miss Bowman had said, "and are doing a great work. Ours is just started, and so of course we have not done much yet; but a few of the most earnest ones from the city are coming out tonight to help us, to interest some of our young people, and to teach them how they do things."

"I'd just as soon my sister wouldn't learn how they do things, if those are Christian Endeavor manners," commented the young man as he thought of her words.

It was a full hour afterward when he walked into the already crowded church, and took a back seat, counting himself favored to get a seat anywhere, as there were already many standing.

Well, certainly the singing was something fine. He must say that in fairness. He had never heard such singing in the Brinton church before. It sounded as if a whole choir of angels had suddenly come down, and were bearing along the voices of the people, and swelling the melody with their own ecstatic music. He felt like joining in himself. Somebody handed him a leaflet with the songs printed on it, and he sang with the rest:

> *"Blessed assurance, Jesus is mine;*
> *O what a foretaste of glory divine!"*

But that was only singing. Worldlings could sing. He could sing himself when there were plenty of other people with voices.

The pastor of the church was asked to pray; and he did so in earnest words and short. Tom, not being a Christian, did not feel himself called upon to bow his heart in prayer with the rest; and so he spent the time listening to the clear-cut sentences woven together so well, and fraught with so much meaning, and was proud that the Brinton minister could compare with any city minister, even if he did not get so large a salary. In his heart was growing a great liking for this new minister, though not as yet for his calling.

Then the president of the Brinton Christian Endeavor Society, a meek, shy boy, who was almost overcome with his position, managed to speak a few awkward words of welcome, which were responded to in fitting words, well chosen and earnest, spoken by one of the elder young men that had come in another car during the ride from the city. But Tom remembered having seen him behind the others as they came along the platform of the city station.

"Well, he knows his business, and speaks sensibly," said the critic. "But then, he is not very young, and you can see by his face that he is sober minded."

There followed several papers by the chairmen of different committees, giving their experiences in the best ways of working.

"We will hear a little account of the Eighth Street lookout committee. They have been remarkably successful this winter in gathering in new members, especially active members; and I'm sure you'll all be interested in hearing how they did it," said the leader of the meeting. "Their chairman, Mr. Fred Pullman, promised to be here, but was detained at the last moment; but one of their members is here, Miss Fanny Welbourne, and she has kindly consented to tell us all about it."

A young girl rose from the center of the house, from among a bevy of boys and girls. Tom Rushmore thought he saw something familiar about her. She was speaking in a clear, well-modulated voice, which sounded sweet and womanly. He looked again, fascinated at once by the first sentence.

"I think the secret of our success was prayer," she was saying. And just then she turned her head so that Tom saw her full in the face — a sweet, bright face, all full of enthusiasm now. It fairly took his breath away, but there was no doubt about it: this was the same girl that he had seen act in so ill-mannered a way on the trip. He could scarcely believe his eyes and ears as she went on.

"We meet twice a month for a little prayer-meeting of our own. Each one of us prays. This was hard work at first; but we have found that it has brought us a great blessing to do so. We pray first for ourselves, and then we pray for the others, the special ones, you know, that are on our list for prayer and help. We have to pray first for ourselves, because we wouldn't be fit to work and pray for the others if our own hearts were not right. Some of us think we have come very close to Jesus in this way, and that he is helping us to do better in our everyday lives. Then each one of us takes someone to pray for especially every day, and to work for all we can. And sometimes this is very hard, when we are asked to take someone we don't like a bit, and we have to forgive the person and pray for ourselves a lot before we can try to do anything for him. We have one member of our committee who is just lovely. She is very unselfish, and she is very Christlike. I think she is the most Christlike person I ever met. She prays for people all the time; and she never has any trouble in doing it, because she never hates anyone. I wish you could have another person just like her here to put on your lookout committee. If she were only here tonight, she would tell you more than I can. I'm just new at this work; but I had to tell you about it, because it has done me so much good, and I thought you would like to know."

Then she sat down, and there was quite a little stir all about her as this one and that leaned over to her with an approving nod or whispered word; and her cheeks were rosy, as if it had been a new experience for her to speak.

Tom Rushmore was amazed. This was a puzzle that he could not unravel. When she began, he had curled his lip in scorn over the idea of that girl's setting up to be "good." Her life did not match her words, he was sure; but as she went on, there was a ring of real earnestness in her tone, which made itself felt in spite of the bad influence of her behavior on the train. Her heedless actions had almost kept one member out of the Christian Endeavor Society, and perhaps out of the church and out of Christ; yet God was allowing her a little chance to undo what evil she had done.

There followed a few moments of prayer, in which many took part, most of them in only one sentence. It was something entirely new and very solemn to Tom Rushmore to hear so many and so young people pray. Something of his old criticism tried to return as he heard and recognized two or three voices that had been loudest on the cars; but something whispered, "They did not know; they did not realize how their actions looked to others. They did no real wrong; it was but your taste they offended. Give them one more chance before you pass judgment on them and on their God, whom they profess to serve and follow."

There was a young girl sitting in a chair in the aisle at the end of young Rushmore's seat. Her face was clear and sweet. There was a wonderful placidity about it, which spoke of a source of joy in her heart. She was beautiful too, and yet had another beauty than that of mere form and feature and complexion. It seemed that a beautiful spirit was dwelling behind that face. He had watched her several times during the evening, thinking that if he were an artist he would like to paint that face, and yet feeling that there was something in it that could never be painted, and wondering what it was and what made it. While Fanny Welbourne was speaking, the girl's face had lighted up with an eager joy, and she had leaned forward and taken in every word. Now, as they were sitting with bowed heads, from behind her shielding hand came the words, so distinctly that they could be heard all over the room, and yet not spoken in a loud tone, "Dear Jesus, we thank thee for what thou hast done for us. Please teach each one of us what it is we most need, and help us to pray for that."

The meeting closed soon after, and Miss Bowman slipped through the crowd to Tom's side.

"Mr. Rushmore, please wait a moment. I want to introduce you to Mr. Eldridge, the city president. I am sure you will like him."

He bowed assent courteously, and stepped out of the aisle to wait. The young girl that had sat at the end of his seat had also stepped aside to wait for her friends, when up rushed Fanny Welbourne, with her impetuous, eager face all aglow.

"O Faith!" she cried, before she was fairly beside her, "I didn't know you were here, or I never, never would have spoken in all this world. I was so frightened when I found you were here, and could have spoken yourself. But I had to, you know. When he asked me, I just couldn't say no, and have nothing said about that wonderful committee that has done me so much good. And I meant you, dear; you know that I did. You're just the center of our whole committee. I just wish I could tell you the good you have done me." Yes, Tom was not mistaken. There were tears in Fanny's gay black eyes. "And you meant me in your prayer. I know you did, didn't you? I need to be taught what I most need. I wish you would help tell me." Then she turned with a bright smile to the young man Will, and greeted him with some funny remark before the beautiful girl had time to reply.

And Tom, standing where he could not help hearing it all, looked at that pure, sweet face, and felt that here was indeed one of those that Miss Bowman had meant when she spoke of those earnest ones that were following Jesus so closely, and wished he knew her, that he might ask her to pray for him also.

Tom Rushmore went home half decided to join the Brinton Christian Endeavor Society in spite of all he had said against it.

It is so seldom that we are given an opportunity to erase an ill-written page that it behooves us to take heed to our writing, lest someday it bring us pain and shame.

The Unknown God

Chapter One

The night was cold and dark. A fine mist was falling, and freezing as it fell, covering everything with a glare of ice. The street lamps made vain attempts to light up their corner of the dark world, only succeeding in throwing a feeble flicker here and there on the treacherous pavements, revealing occasional glazed patches of dirty snow in sheltered corners. Even the electric lights which flung their brightness into the night here and there could not give a cheerful air to the city. The streetcar drivers, muffled from head to foot, stood solemnly at their posts, as though performing the world's funeral service. Their gaunt beasts, with not enough spirit left to shiver back at the chilling atmosphere which infolded their heavy bodies, strained at their heavy load, and slipped on the icy stones. All gave one more touch of dreariness to the scene. It was not a night when one would have chosen to take a walk for pleasure; and yet one young man was out with the intention of getting some amusement if it were possible. He was a stranger in the city, having drifted there that very day, and for want of money had engaged himself to work in the first position he could find, which happened to be in the shop of a tobacconist. The work was not altogether to his liking. He was capable of better things. But better things did not present themselves, and he needed money, so he tried to make the best of this.

But it was a poor best that he could make out of it so far. He had to go to a boarding-house, and the cheapest he could find was very cheap in comforts as well as name. He was obliged to take a room with another young man, which he did not like. The room looked dirty, too, and this newcomer was used to a clean room. His mother had been his former landlady; and though she was weary and overworked, still she had contrived to keep things tolerably clean, even if it was but a cheap boarding-house, with an air of unmistakable forlornity and poverty about it. Her son had never paid his board, and consequently had been able to attend theaters and entertainments as often as he chose. It had really never occurred to him that he ought to pay his board to his mother. He gave her money now and then, a little, when she was in a tight place and mustered courage to ask for it. But he enjoyed his evenings at the theater, and a young man ought to have amusement. Perhaps it was in consequence of late hours that he had a habit of sleeping late mornings. He was often behind time at the store, which at last drew down upon him the reproaches of his employer. At this he had grown angry, taken his wages, bought a ticket to this city, and here he was. He thought of it all now as he walked slowly along the city street. He was not exactly sorry yet, though things looked very uncomfortable. He had not analyzed the matter, and therefore did not realize that his love of amusement was perhaps at the bottom of the whole trouble. Indeed, he was on his way to find amusement now, though he had not a cent in his pocket with which to buy a ticket into anything. He was not sufficiently familiar with the city to know in what direction to go; but his instincts told him, and he presently found himself in the region of the large theaters.

An unusually bright flood of light attracted his attention to a large building, and he quickened his steps somewhat. Other people were going in the same direction; for, as he neared the corner, he saw a procession of bobbing umbrellas, and people carefully picking their way along the slippery sidewalk. Something very attractive must be going on here, he felt sure. He joined the crowd, and pressed nearer the door. Over the heads of the people he caught a few glimpses of large letters, just a word or two, "Bernhardt" and "La Tosca."

His heart warmed within him. He had seen Bernhardt before, and knew that "La Tosca" was considered one of her very best parts.

"Now, Brad Benedict, this is just your luck," he muttered to himself as he stood back on the steps and let the crowd surge by him. "I wish I hadn't paid for that miserable week's board in advance. I might have found some place where they wouldn't require that."

This young man, Bradley Benedict, as he stood there in the partial darkness scowling at his fate, had anything but an attractive look; and yet, seen in a strong light, his face was not altogether a poor one. He had a good forehead. It would have been called an intellectual forehead if the rest of his face had not been so utterly out of harmony with such a thought. It was not a weak face, but rather an ungoverned, lawless one. A good thought, or sometimes a glance at his mother, had been known to quite alter his expression, until he had almost a look of goodness and beauty. But he had a quick temper and a headstrong will.

By his side stepped an old gentleman, leaning forward in the light, fumbling with some coins, evidently trying to find one of the right value with which to pay for an evening paper he had just bought, and which a small newsboy was holding impatiently up to him. Three ladies, who seemed to belong to the old gentleman, waited a little apart. Suddenly, with a nervous move, the old gentleman dropped his wallet at the feet of the young man, scattering coins this way and that. There was much good nature in young Benedict's make-up, and he instantly stooped to help the old gentleman. But when the wallet was finally righted and the newsboy paid, the old man seemed disturbed, and still searched the dark steps eagerly.

"There's an odd bit of coin missing that I picked up in my travels; I wouldn't lose it for a good deal," he said in a troubled tone.

Bradley began the search once more, and after some minutes he rescued the coin from a crack into which it had slipped.

The old gentleman's thanks were profuse, and he seemed to be looking the young man over to see if it would do to offer to pay him for the service performed. But Bradley had worn his best clothes when he came off on this expedition to a strange city, and the old man decided that it would not do. Suddenly a new thought struck him.

"Have you a ticket in here, young man?" he asked.

"No," growled Benedict, recalling his misfortune once more.

"Well, I've an extra one that our party won't use. Take it if you want it. Hope you'll enjoy it. I'm obliged to you for your service."

He pressed the ticket into Bradley's hand, and was gone. The young man did not wait long, but followed his benefactor up the steps and into the hall, very much pleased with the change in his fortunes.

He presented his ticket, and was shown to his seat, which proved to be a good one, but not near the seat of the old gentleman. Of that he was glad. He felt more self-respect here, as if he had paid his own way in. He settled himself, and began to look about. The opera house was a fine one, and there was much of interest to be seen; but his attention was almost immediately directed to the stage. It presented a remarkable appearance to the eyes of this young man who was so accustomed to attend the theater. There were seats built up in semi-circular tiers which nearly covered it, and the curtain was raised. What in the world did it mean? While he looked, there filed in several hundred people, musicians with their great instruments and ladies in beautiful dresses, and seated themselves.

It certainly was something new under the sun. He was not aware that Bernhardt performed with any such chorus, but perhaps "La Tosca" introduced new features.

Presently there came in two young women dressed more in the theater style than any of the others, followed by two young men in full evening dress, with another handsome young man a little in the rear. At sight of them the audience broke into applause.

"Who are they?" Benedict ventured to ask the young man at his side.

"The soloists and the leader," replied his neighbor in a tone which made the questioner feel like a greenhorn, and resolve to keep his mouth closed.

Above the hum of talk arose the soft murmur and twang of the different instruments as their owners tightened a string here and there. The scene and the sounds were much like the opening of any performance, with the exception of the well-filled stage. He tried to think that there was still another stage beyond this one, and that presently the curtain, which represented a road winding off to green hills, with lovely woods on either side, would roll up and disclose it, but he came to the conclusion, after a little study, that this was impossible. He looked the audience over. It was much like the audience of a high-class opera. The boxes near the stage were filled with people, many of them in full dress and ablaze with diamonds. He had heard that Bernhardt drew the elite. He watched the different people as they came in. Some wore quiet dress; but the large majority of those who took seats in the parquet and dress circle carried their wraps in their hands, or thrown loosely about their shoulders, and wore no hats. As he watched, an old lady with white hair drawn into many wearying puffs and crimps, with a long white opera cloak enveloping her stout figure, rolled by him, followed by her footman with most decorous bearing. A man with a tall crush hat, an eyeglass, and a fur-trimmed overcoat reaching from his hat-brim to his toes, followed and made much display in seating himself, and arranging his belongings to his satisfaction.

As young Benedict was absorbed in looking at these (to him) odd specimens of humanity, and making mental comments upon them, there suddenly broke upon his ear a soft, sweet strain, so low and tender that it could scarcely have been distinguished had there not been an instant hush in the audience to let the beautiful music flow over it. He did not remember having ever watched a fine orchestra before. It was very interesting, and to a certain extent the wonderful sweetness of the music thrilled him. He glanced angrily at a group of belated ones in the aisle who were waiting for this to be over that they might be seated, and who were heartless enough to whisper; and it fell sharply upon his ear when some irate individual upon whom the door had been closed rapped loudly several times for admittance. He glared at an usher, and wondered why such things were not stopped. The music had certainly found a little entrance-way into his soul, although he was looking for something very much more to his taste; while this was going on, he wanted to hear it.

He drew a long breath as the music died away. Music never made him feel so strange before, and he did not understand it.

There was a moment's pause, during which people rustled into seats, and then a rich, sweet tenor sang clear and distinct the words: "Comfort ye my people, saith your God." In all his experience of operas and theaters Bradley Benedict had never heard one that commenced in this way. He wished he knew the idea of this "La Tosca." Could it be that it was a religious play? No; for he had heard it spoken of in anything but a reverent tone.

Chapter Two

Perhaps there was sarcasm behind it all. Maybe the curtain would rise in a moment, and a great chorus would break in above this sweet voice, and drown it, and there would be cheers and laughter and something jolly. But this thought grated. He did not want the sweet voice stopped. Something in these words appealed to him.

They were so distinctly spoken that he could not but understand; and yet, though he heard, his mind took in but that first sentence of the solo: "Comfort ye my people, saith your God."

Comfort. He knew what that meant. He dimly remembered how in his little boyhood, when he fell or hurt his finger, his mother would drop everything and gather him up in her arms, and say, "Mother will comfort you." He suddenly felt how utterly desolate he was here in this strange city, and that he would like to be a little boy again, with his mother to comfort him. To be sure, it was long years since that mother had had time or strength to think of comforting her son; and if she had, she would about as soon have thought of offering comfort to the president of the United States as to him, for she would not have expected it to be received with anything but scorn. But the grown-up boy dimly remembered the comfort and shelter of those arms long ago, and had a faint desire to feel them about him once more.

"Comfort my people, *saith your God*," the song rang on. Did God care to comfort people? What would be such comfort if a mother's were so good? What was God? It was a new picture to this darkened mind, the picture of a God comforting beloved people; and the outlines were dim for the reason that there was too much brightness in it for these eyes so long unused to the light.

"Every valley shall be exalted, and every mountain and hill made low, the crooked straight, and the rough places plain," sang on the same voice; and Bradley did not understand it. He looked for the curtain to rise and explain all; but, instead, the chorus rose, and burst forth in one grand prophetic strain: "And the glory of the Lord shall be revealed, and all flesh shall see it together; for the mouth of the Lord hath spoken it." The singers took up the sentence, and shouted it back and forth at one another with a gladness in their voices that made this one listener feel that they were speaking of something which brought them pleasure; and in some way there was a little thrill of satisfaction in his own heart, so used to respond with emotion to what was put before him in song, or act, or story. This certainly was a different theater. A deep bass voice now took up the song in solemn accents:

"Thus saith the Lord of hosts. Yet once a little while, and I will shake the heavens and the earth, and the sea and the dry land, and I will shake all nations. . . . The Lord whom ye seek shall suddenly come to his temple, even the messenger of the covenant, whom ye delight in."

Could it be that these people were going to dare to produce all this in scenery and acting? Would they try to have an earthquake and a storm at sea? Would they try to represent the coming of the Lord? This young man was shocked at the thought. His idea of God had never been a very definite one. He had been to Sunday school when he was a small boy; but the teacher had been one who did not approve of trying to teach much of sacred things to little children, so he had a general idea that he must be good, or a great and terrible Being would do something awful to him. When he graduated from this class, the teacher required him to learn a lesson, and he thought it stupid, so he stayed away. His mother, poor thing, had not known much of God, or at least had not tried to teach him. He had heard God's name mostly taken in vain; indeed, he had not been altogether careful of using it himself upon occasion. Why should he? It meant little to him. And yet, the thought that this terrible song about the Lord's sudden coming was about to be represented, jarred him —

frightened him, perhaps. He looked about upon the audience, to see if any one felt as he did; but they all looked calm. One lady was intently studying the scrap of a butterfly bonnet on the head of her neighbor in front; and the eyeglass man had his neck twisted to get a better view of someone in a private box, through his opera glasses. Bradley wondered vaguely how they could be so indifferent. Did people know what this was to be? He had heard that many people objected to the play of "La Tosca"; and perhaps it was as he feared. But the grand voice went calmly on, speaking the terrible words:

"But who may abide the day of his coming; and who shall stand when he appeareth? For he is like a refiner's fire."

Bradley heard no more for some time. His heart was stirred wonderfully. This was awful. He wished the old man on the street had not dropped his wallet, nor given him the ticket. He wished he was out in the cold and sleet this very minute. He would get out of this. It was a terrible place; how people stood it he did not understand. But everything was still, everyone listening. He did not want to make a stir, and draw all eyes to himself. Perhaps when this solo was finished there would be a pause, when he could get out. Meantime, he tried to stop his ears from hearing these terrible words. Nevertheless, they sounded all the clearer in his heart, and he began to wonder how he could stand before this God whom he knew not.

The young man, his neighbor, looked at him curiously as he wriggled uneasily in his seat, glancing back toward the door, and a good woman at his other side offered him her fan; but his discomfort grew. He looked down at his boots, trying to forget the hall, and all about him; think of what he would do on the morrow; lay plans for his future career. And the people in the hall seemed to silently troop away for a while, the seats seemed to be empty, and left him alone with the voice; and swiftly there gathered about him, in shadowy forms, the acts of his past life, and looked down upon him trembling, as the voice died away in the words: "For he is like a refiner's fire."

The contralto had taken up the song; but the change of voice did not arrest the attention of the young man. He seemed under a spell. He heard none of the words of the solo except the closing — so soft and sweet that it fell like a blessing on the hushed roof: "Emmanuel, God with us." It left a tender touch in the air as it died away. There was gladness almost too deep for utterance in the voice of the singer; and yet this must be the God about whom the question had been asked: "Who shall stand when he appeareth?"

There were some, then, to whom the thought: "God with us," brought nothing but wonderful joy! What a God was this!

The joyous-voiced chorus took up the strain: "O thou that tellest good tidings to Zion, get thee up into the high mountain."

Bradley looked up; the shadows slunk behind, and the audience was there again. It was impossible not to be lifted up by this burst of joy and melody, though the young man did not understand in the least what it all was about. There seemed no sense or connection; and yet he dimly perceived the story running through the whole, as one who listens to a tale in an unknown tongue, and understanding not one single connected sentence, will yet catch at the sense from the speaker's voice or motions, or from the lighting of the eyes, so subtle are the ways that spirits have of communicating thoughts to one another.

"Arise, shine, for thy light has come, and the glory of the Lord is risen upon thee." And this listener felt his soul try to rise and be glad with the rest; but the bonds of its ignorance and blindness were so great that it sank back again in despair. He felt the cold, chill shadows creep over the earth, and darkness so dense it could be felt hiding every face, as the bass told the story. Then gradually there lifted a corner of this heavy blackness, and a little light crept into the sky as the voice went on: "The people that walked in darkness have seen a great light." And there came an eager anxiety in his heart to see that light, and stand in the full rays of its brightest glory, even as he had sometimes longed to be the great, rich, successful hero of some play to which he had listened for an evening, only there was something different about this feeling that swayed him. It was so dim and indefinite and far away, and only part of him seemed to long for this, while the other part of himself was angry and irritated at the thought, and wished to get away. Why didn't he go? But the chorus was rising again. He would go as soon as they were through; the room was too still now.

Softly as an angel might have sung above a sleeping baby, the music began. The great company of sopranos hushed their sweet notes till they sounded far away in the clouds; then coming nearer, tenderly, exultantly, yet as if there might be tears in the voices — tears of joy — came the words: "For unto us a child is born."

And the basses took it up in the same faraway tone, as though it floated from an upper world almost: "Unto us a son is given."

Still a third time the altos sang the strain, and a fourth the tenors took it up. They were all glad, and was this poor, bound soul of his to have no part in the joy? And what was it all about? A child born! A son given! And why should they all care about that?

"And the government shall be upon his shoulder, and his name — shall be call—ed" — sang the whole company, and then paused an instant for the orchestra to catch up, and gather strength to bring out the words that followed — wonderful words, like great, polished precious stones of many colors and greatest brilliancy, which shone in the setting of this golden music as if placed there by a master work-man.

"Wonderful!"

Bradley Benedict sat up straight, his hands clinched, and his breath scarcely coming through his tightly closed lips. He had never heard a word spoken or sung like that before.

"Counselor!"

A great wave seemed to sweep over him, and roll away, leaving him breathless.

"The mighty God!"

Every syllable seemed to strike a great blow at his heart, and go through him, and a fear came stealing over it. But there was something like a benediction in the next: "The everlasting Father!"

Now, in spite of fear, there came a longing for his mother again. He did not remember his father's love.

"The Prince of peace!" sang the great company, who seemed to have been coming on and on, until now they were here in their full power; and the chorus sat down amid loud applause. The noise of it seemed harsh and out of place to the heart that had just been so stirred by the grandeur of the music. He wished the people had kept still.

And now the orchestra broke away as though the heavenly company had just come down to sing this one song, and announce to earth this one great thing, and were hastening back to join the praise in heaven.

Very sweet the strains were, and Bradley

listened as he had never listened to any music in his life before. He did not know it was called a pastoral symphony, and would not have known what that was if he had been told. He only knew he liked it, and was annoyed extremely when a lady behind him sneezed a funny little catlike sneeze just in the midst of it, which set two young girls in the row in front to giggling.

This music seemed to have in it suggestions of all that had been left out of his life — clear skies, and sunny days, and the hushed, sweet peace of green fields far away from city life. He had never known that he cared for these things, but now they stood like beautiful, inviting pictures. He could even hear the murmur of the night wind as it whispered among tall branches, and softly touched tired grass and sleeping flowers, humming a little in tune with a twinkling brook which wound about not far away. The birds seemed all asleep; he thought he heard one twitter as he stirred. The world, the noisy world, seemed a long way off from this quiet place, where all were waiting for some great thing to happen. The meadows were not all alone with the birds. He, Bradley Benedict, the new hand at rolling tobacco, was there. He was awfully conscious of his own presence in that holy place the music was picturing. There were others waiting too. Indeed, he was not sure if the whole world were not waiting with him to see what would happen.

Now the soprano was singing in simple, clear recitative about the shepherds abiding in the fields, keeping watch over their flocks by night. Bradley could see the night sky, with its dotting of stars, and the glory that suddenly shone; could see the angel when he came, and the shepherds' faces. The story was all very new to him. Scarce any inkling of it had ever reached his brain before. Christmas had not brought its revelation to him as to many others. His childish idea of that day had been measured by the amount of property he acquired in sticks of candy, sleds, and balls.

When the tender air of "He shall feed his flock like a shepherd" floated through the room, there was something so infinitely lovely and loving in this One described, that his heart went out in longing in spite of himself; and when the soprano took up the song, with "Come unto him, all ye that labor and are heavy laden, and he will give you rest," there were almost tears in his eyes; he could scarcely control himself, and he had a strong conviction that if that One about whom they were singing stood up there where he could see him, inviting him, he would have to go. He would not be strong enough to resist.

The intermission had come. The young leader turned, bowing to the audience, then sank into his chair, throwing back his hair, and wiping his forehead with his handkerchief. Benedict might leave now. Why did he not take this opportunity? Others were going out. The fat old lady with the white head and white cloak was lumbering out, with her dignified footman gravely following, bearing robes and shawls. She looked bored. The young man had lost his desire to get out; but half mechanically he reached down for his hat, until a remark of a pretty girl nearby attracted his attention to the leader.

"He looks awfully tired, doesn't he? My! He must be smart to have drilled them so well."

"Yes; and he's so graceful," murmured her companion. "But it's a dreadfully long program, I think. He ought to leave out some."

Bradley's eyes went to the leader, who looked not much older than himself. The face was noble, pure, and intellectual. He could but admire it. What was this young man?

Why did he give such a strange performance? Bradley had long ago made up his mind that Sarah Bernhardt would not appear this evening. He had made some mistake. But what *was* this to which he had come? Did this young man feel and believe all the singing he had been leading? Or was it mere poetry? No, Bradley decided that it was something higher than mere sentiment. He made up his mind that the young man felt the joy of belonging to that everlasting Father. If he did not, how could he have made those people sing it with such triumphant voices, as if they were the angels themselves, come down to tell the story?

But the intermission was over, and he had not gone yet, albeit his hat was in his hand.

The chorus had begun once more.

"Behold the Lamb of God, that taketh away the sins of the world."

He began to long to have his own sins taken away, and wonder how it could be done; and when the sad contralto voice began to sing he listened eagerly.

"He was despised and rejected of men; a man of sorrows, and acquainted with grief." And then the chorus: "Surely he hath borne our griefs, and carried our sorrows. He was wounded for our transgressions; he was bruised for our iniquities: the chastisement of our peace was upon him, and with his stripes we are healed. All we like sheep have gone astray."

"Have gone astray," echoed the alto, and bass and tenor answered, too, "We have gone astray; we have turned every one to his own way."

"Yes; we have turned every one to his own way," answered the listening heart that now thought of it for the first time. He had turned to his own way when he left his old employer and his mother, and came off here to this strange city to seek his fortune, which was proving so hard to find. He began to see many other things he had done and left undone. How *he* had turned to his own way.

"And the Lord hath laid on him the iniquity of us all."

There was something almost terrible in the sweetness of this concluding sentence. What claim had he upon the great Lord that his iniquity should be laid upon him? During the first part he had been terrified and discomfited because, in the light of the prophecies, he had been made to see his own heart more clearly than he had ever seen it before; and now, when his own worthlessness and sin stood out so blackly, here was a pitying One ready to take the whole. He began to understand the story better, which at first had seemed so utterly incomprehensible. But what was this the tenor was singing?

"Thy rebuke hath broken his heart. He is full of heaviness. He looked for some to have pity on him, but there was no man, neither found he any to comfort him. Behold, and see if there be any sorrow like unto his sorrow."

He bowed his head in his hands, regardless of the curious and scornful neighbor. What did it mean? There must be love to make such sorrow, and all for him — that is, for the world, and he realized that he was included. Could it be that there was in the heart of this young man at that moment a little thrill of real love for the unknown God who had borne sorrow for him, and with none to comfort him? With none to comfort him! Again that strange little thrill in his heart! Here was a link between himself and this God. Had he not longed for comfort that very night? His mind went back to the first words of the evening: "Comfort ye my people, saith your God." God who had been without comfort or pity in his own great sorrow, yet wanted the people who had caused this sorrow to be comforted! It was *wonderful.* It was not strange that that word, one of his names, had rung out so clear and strong and bright in the music. "Wonderful!" Such a God as this was indeed wonderful!

When he raised his head again, the chorus was singing: "Lift up your heads, O ye gates, and be ye lifted up, ye everlasting doors, and the King of glory shall come in."

And the great question which seemed to be asked by many of all nations and ages, "Who is the King of glory?" was the same question he had asked himself at the beginning of the evening. Who was this God? The answer swelled and soared as from millions of voices besides those belonging to the visible chorus on the platform: "The Lord strong and mighty, the Lord mighty in battle. The Lord of hosts, he is the King of glory."

Some little idea of the power and majesty meant to be conveyed by these words entered this newly aroused mind, and he pondered over the thought that such a mighty God should care for him.

He was absorbed in this idea for some time, and did not take in what followed, until suddenly, with one accord, quietly and respectfully, the whole audience rose to their feet! Benedict got up too, just as the first great "hallelujah" of that magnificent chorus burst upon his ears. Astonished at all that had gone before, worn out with the unusual emotions that had been swelling within his heart, trembling from excitement so that he could scarcely stand, he listened as the hallelujahs were flung on every side with prodigal hand, like resplendent rockets in a great celebration; and his heart swelled as the words of adoration were poured forth from those hundreds of trained throats: "King of kings, and Lord of lords! Hallelujah!" and felt that he could never go back to his old life, and be the same again.

He was dimly conscious that there followed this another intermission, during which time a great many of the diamonded and eyeglassed sort rustled out, and their places were quietly and gladly filled from the throng which had paid for standing room at the back of the house.

Of the third part which followed, he remembered only the first solo, that wonderful sentence, the climax of our trust, which contains our hope for life eternal:

"I know that my Redeemer liveth, and that he shall stand at the latter day upon the earth; and though worms destroy this body, yet in my flesh shall I see God. For now is Christ risen from the dead, the firstfruits of them that sleep."

Oh, to know that! To feel that wonderful surety! He looked at the white-robed singer with awe, feeling almost the possibility that she might vanish from their sight into the heavens when this song was over. It never entered his mind but that she felt it all; how else could she sing so to other hearts?

The closing triumphal chorus he heard as in a dream; but he echoed the "blessing and honor, glory and power, for ever and ever," with a glad "Amen" in his heart, keeping in his mind all the while the words, "I know," and resolving that they should be his own someday if ever he could find out how to make them his.

He went out into the dark and wet.

Chapter Three

The rain had almost ceased; the wind was keener and sharper, and the pavements had become treacherous glass indeed. The throng ahead of him slipped and tottered, and some actually fell. They had to fairly crawl along; but Bradley Benedict heeded none of these things. He was back in the opera house still, face to face with the Man of sorrows; and he scarcely noted which way he was going until a hand was laid upon his shoulder, and a voice, which was altogether too familiar to please him, shouted, "Hello! Which way you goin', and where you bin?"

It was the young man who was to be his roommate, on his way from a cheap theater. He knew the look of the place. He had been to such often before, and taken delight in them; but tonight his heart turned from it with revulsion. He felt as if he had lived years since he entered the opera house that evening.

"I'm going home," he answered his companion shortly; and even as he spoke he felt what a misnomer that word was when applied to the squalid lodging house. He wished he were going home to his mother; and then and there he resolved to go just as soon as he could earn enough to take him.

"H'm!" said the other young man. "Well, you'd better turn around and plod along in the other direction if you expect to get there without going around the world. Come on!" and he turned his unwilling friend about, and, linking his arm in his, walked along by his side.

"Wher've you been?" he asked Benedict presently, as soon as they were out of the worst of the crowd.

"In there," said Benedict, pointing toward the great opera house with a sort of friendly feeling for the building where he had passed through such a strange experience. There was a glow in his heart which he could not understand.

"There!" exclaimed the other in a surprised voice. "You must have a heap of cash. It costs a penny to get in there. What's on tonight? Bernhardt? Let me see. No. Why, it was the oratorio night, wasn't it?" He glanced up at his companion with astonishment and a look almost of respect. "Is that the set you belong to?" he added, as Benedict replied simply by a nod. He had never known exactly what an oratorio was before; but now that he considered the matter, it certainly must have been what he had been listening to.

It was a silent walk the rest of the way to the boarding-house. Benedict's mind was too full of other things to care to talk much, and the young man by his side found he had no conversation ready for the sort of companion who took his amusement at the oratorio *Messiah*. Now and then he glanced curiously at him as they shuffled along over the ice. A keen, strong wind had risen, and afforded sufficient excuse for them to retire behind their coat collars and keep silence.

Bradley Benedict was turning over in his mind this thought: Would this strange, new feeling stay with him, or would it go away and leave his life the same empty void, without purpose or promise, that it had been but a few hours before? He realized now that it had been a bad and worthless life, and wondered at himself for never knowing it before.

Sleep did not come to this young man so soon as to his roommate. The air of the room was breathless; and mingled with the smell of tobacco there was a strong odor of fried onions, lingering probably from the boarding-house supper. His evening in company with refined people, listening to wonderful music, and thinking higher thoughts than had ever entered his mind before, seemed to have quickened his sensibilities to these little things. He felt almost stifled. He arose, went to the window, and threw up the sash. The cold air poured

in, and made him shiver; but he threw his
coat about his shoulders and looked out.
The city was quieting into its after-mid-
night stillness now; the breeze had blown a
small space in the heavy sky for the moon
to shine faintly through, which the hurry-
ing clouds were rapidly trying to cover
again. One tiny star threw out a few flickering, straggling beams between clouds.
The earth looked very dark, save where the
lights of the city shone through glass. It
was intensely cold. The sky grew black
again as the clouds gained a temporary victory over the moon and the one star.
Bradley felt alone — alone with God, and
"Who shall stand when he appeareth?"
came to his mind. Then the moon strug-
gled through the clouds once more, and he
thought of the words: "The people that sat
in darkness have seen a great light." How
many scraps of song he could remember!
He felt the same desires which had moved
him when he first heard the words — the
longing to be able to sing the joyful songs;
to feel secure; to have this Friend, this
Comforter. Suddenly, as if in answer to his
soul's cry, there seemed to come over the
wicked city a soft, sweet voice singing the
words with tender pathos: "Come unto
me, all ye that labor and are heavy laden,

and I will give you rest."

He listened until the voice died away on the night, and then in the darkness he bowed his head, and came and found rest.

Mrs. Benedict sat by the remains of a meager fire in the grate of the "parlor," as it was called. The room was deserted by all the boarders now, and she was free to sit here in peace for a few minutes. It was very late, and she was weary — so weary that she had scarcely strength to take her up the stairs to her sleeping room. She had thought earlier in the day that the most delightful thing that could happen to her would be to drop into a bed and stay there, and never have to get up again. She had gone through the day with an almost eager looking forward to the time when she could throw her burdensome tired-out body on the bed, and relax the overstrained muscles for a little time. But here she sat, trying to warm herself from the few weak-looking coals still left in the grate, and gain strength to go up to her room. It had been a more than usually wearisome day. The cook had been undeniably drunk, and not able to do a stroke of work; and the slouchy second girl, who was her only other assistant, had been out late the night before, and had done nothing all day but dawdle about and yawn. One of the young men boarders, who she had hoped would turn out to be a "permanent," had left that morning; another had departed, leaving a used-up pair of suspenders, and a hat with the crown jammed in, to pay his last month's board. She had decidedly failed in her meek efforts to coax three others into paying something toward past arrears; and the rent collector had called, and told her that he could not wait much longer. Besides all this, she had the neuralgia in one cheek and eye — and her boy was gone away. That was the climax. Her boy! She had thought about it and cried about it until she had no more strength left for either. As she sat looking absently into the coals, where smoldered the stumps of two or three boarders' cigars, a tear trickled weakly down her cheek, scarcely gathering strength enough as it went to fall in a good honest splash in her lap, but spreading itself out in a wet spot among the wrinkles. Her hair was rough and gray; and one lock had escaped from the pin that tried to hold it in a hard knot at the back of her head, and hung now in a discouraged way about her face. The eyes were faded blue, and the skin was so wrinkled you could not guess what the contour of the face might have been in earlier days. She looked a sad picture of despair.

The room itself was a desolate enough place. Mrs. Benedict had been obliged to relax her vigilance for cleanliness during the trials of the past few days; and, as a consequence, the disorder that reigned made it even more Sahara-like than usual. The ashes had spread themselves about on the hearth, and gathered a small collection of toothpicks and cigar stumps. A fine, soft dust was over the mantel, broken here and there by the marks of some boarder's elbow.

There was an emaciated, hollow-chested, haircloth sofa against the wall; a table on the other side of the room, with a faded red-and-black flannel spread, and holding a few *"Fireside Companions."* A weary-faced clock on the mantel, a few cane-seat chairs in various stages of dilapidation, and a depressed-looking rocker, completed the furniture of the room. The floor was covered with a large-figured, much faded and darned red-and-green ingrain carpet, helped out in front of door and fireplace by pieces of dreary oilcloth from which the paint had long ago departed. On the walls hung a few family groups and portraits,

Mrs. Benedict's marriage certificate, and a cross made of hair flowers, all framed in oval or square black frames.

The marriage certificate occupied the place of honor over the sofa, with a full-length portrait of "Braddie," as she called her son, hanging on one side. He wore baggy plaid trousers that looked full enough for a modern divided skirt, white stockings, a high white collar, and a very short coat, and carried a hat, much too old and large for him, stiffly in one hand. The hair was long and thick, and the face chunky and expressionless, for the photograph was a poor one, and old; but his mother gazed at him, remembered her little boy as he used to be, and sighed a great, deep sigh. Then she turned her tear-dimmed eyes to the picture which hung on the other side. It was a man, presumably, though the picture, which must have been taken long ago, had faded so that little was distinct save some black hair and a coat. The light from the smoky lamp was turned low, however, and there was no bright fire to help out the features. But the lonely heart looking at them knew how the face had looked, and the weak tears gathered and coursed down between their wrinkles thick and fast. It was a hard world, and she was so tired!

A sharp ring of the doorbell broke the stillness of the room, and she looked toward the hall a moment in surprise. Yes, she had locked the door for the night before sitting down. Surely all the boarders were in. The clerk at Mason's came in half an hour ago, and he was always the last one. But she arose mechanically, and went to answer the bell.

She unfastened the lock, and threw back the door, holding the lamp in one hand in front of her eyes, so that she was completely blinded. While the darkness rushed in, and the lamplight staggered out to take its place, she was conscious of somebody standing beside her. It was a strong man like her Braddie. He shut the door, took the lamp from her hand, and then, taking her in his arms, uttered one word: "Mother!"

She was so tired and so glad, and there was a confusion in her mind whether this was really Braddie, or Braddie's father come back to earth again, he seemed so like his father as he held her. She had not been held so for twenty years.

To his old employer Bradley Benedict said the next morning, "I've found God, Mr. Bolton; and I've come home to take care of my mother and prove to you that

303

I'm trying to live a different life, if you'll take me back and try me."

It was two or three years afterward when it was announced that the oratorio *Messiah* would be rendered in the largest church of the place in which the Benedicts lived. Bradley immediately took two tickets, and selected the best seats the house afforded. Then he said, "Mother, the oratorio *Messiah* is to be here next week, and I want you to hear it. It is what saved me, and brought me home to begin life over again."

And Mrs. Benedict, not in the least knowing what an oratorio was, but glad to please "her Braddie," donned her plain black silk, and combed her white hair to its smoothest, and went. She sat and watched her tall boy proudly through the whole evening, and told him at the close it was a nice concert, as good as any she and his father ever went to. But of the music she heard little, and she wondered in her heart what it could possibly be in that singing which had anything to do with Bradley's coming home.

Things have changed since Bradley Benedict came home that night. The boarders are gone, and the family has moved to a small, cozy house. The old furniture has given place to bright, cheery belongings, and Mrs. Benedict is renewing her youth under the loving care of her son.

Oh, ye disciples of Fashion and Art, as I passed by and beheld your devotions, I found an altar, in this oratorio *Messiah*, set up by you "To the Unknown God." Whom therefore ye ignorantly worship, him could this unlearned young man declare unto you. For God, "that made the world and all things therein, and hath made of one blood all nations for to dwell on all the face of the earth, and hath determined the times before appointed, and the bounds of their habitation; that they should seek the Lord, if haply they might feel after him, and find him, though he be not far from every one of us."

Under the Window

The little bronze clock on the shelf over the fireplace chimed out seven, and then took up its next hour's work of counting out the seconds to the sleeping cat on the hearth. The room was all alone, and very still, having a quiet time by itself. The fire winked and blinked at the lamp, and the lamp beamed brightly back from under its homemade shade of rose-colored tissue paper and cardboard. The carpet, a neat ingrain, looked as if it knew its place and what was expected of it — namely, to look prettier than it really was, to wear long and not show dirt — and it would not presume upon its privileges even when the mistress was out. The sofa was wide, deep, and comfortable, made of a dry-goods box, with a wide board nailed on for a back, and the whole deftly padded and covered with an old crimson shawl, with fringes too shabby to be used any longer as an outside wrap.

There were curtains too. You wouldn't have had them in your room. They were nothing but cheesecloth with rows of threads pulled and tied; but they were cheap, and gave a pretty air of grace and homeliness to the room. Besides, they were held back from the windows by broad yellow satin ribbons. To be sure, the ribbons were only old pink ones, washed and dyed with diamond dye; but they were yellow, and added a dainty touch to the plainness of other things.

There was a small table with a red cover, which held the lamp; two wooden chairs, a little rocker covered with cretonne, and a stool near the hearth. Above the table was a little shelf with a Bible and a few other books.

The only really elegant things in the room were the bronze clock and two delicate vases of Parian marble; but these were presents from some former little pupils of the mistress, and, as such, occupied the place of honor — the broad shelf over the wide, old-fashioned fireplace. But they seemed to have made friends with the ingrain carpet, the homemade sofa, and the cheesecloth curtains, and to feel quite as much at home with the yellow ribbons as though the latter had been real and new, not old and dyed. There were a few pictures and bright cards that smiled down from the walls — and the room kept very still and waited, all alone. Now and again the white cat stirred in his sleep, opened one eye up at the clock, as though he had just heard it strike those seven clear strokes, pushed his forepaws slowly, tremblingly forward, in the luxury of a stretch, opened his mouth to its utmost extent, then turned over to cuddle down again, one paw over his nose, and a contented smile on his pink cat mouth.

There were two windows in the room, one looking out on the little strip of ground between the house and the street, the other opening to a sort of lane or alley; and this window was down from the top several inches, for the mistress had ideas on ventilation. The wind came in and stirred the curtains, even waving the least mite the white fur on the end of the cat's tail; but the cat was used to drafts, and did not mind. He only gave his ear a little nervous jerk, as if he fancied it were summer, and a fly were biting him; though he knew better if he had only stopped to think, for here was the fire, and outside was the snow blowing, and the breath of air that had touched his tail was decidedly cold. There were other reasons too. His mistress had not taken that pile of books and started off to school for three whole days. By that he knew it was the winter vacation. Then, had not old Mr. and Mrs. Updike, from whom he and his mistress rented their rooms, gone away that very morning to spend the holidays with their daughter Hepzibah? The cat and his mistress were alone in the house, except for Peter Kelly, who was probably at that moment sitting in his room over the kitchen, his chair tilted back against the wall, and looking straight at the spluttering flame of his candle.

And why didn't his mistress go away to spend the holidays, and not stay all the happy Christmastide shut up in her little room with her cat? Well, in the first place, she couldn't afford to go away. She was just a poor little schoolteacher, with a very small salary, barely enough to support herself and her cat; for a cat she would have, she said, if she had to go without something herself. Second, she couldn't leave her cat. Who would take care of it? Not Mrs. Updike, for she hated cats; and besides, she was not at home. Third, she had nowhere to go; and so she stayed at home. She had told the white cat only a few days ago that she was all alone in the world, and had dropped a bright tear on his pink ear, and he had twitched his head in surprise.

She was no worse off in that respect than he was, and he was contented. He saw no further need for anyone in the world besides himself and her, except, perhaps, the milkman.

But at that moment the front door opened and closed with a bang: there was a sound of stamping and brushing in the hall; then the mistress entered, and the room seemed to smile and brighten to receive her. Bright brown eyes, golden brown hair, straight nose, cheeks glowing with the cold and exercise, straight eyebrows, and small brown hands — that is Polly Bronson. She wore a dark-blue flannel dress, a black jersey coat, black mittens, and a little black crocheted cap with balls on the top. The snowflakes glistened over all. She shook them gaily off, laid her parcels on the table, and went to hang up her things in the small bedroom adjoining. Coming back, she seated herself on the little stool, and proceeded to poke the fire, making it blaze up brightly.

"Come here, Abbott," she said merrily, "while I tell you the news."

The cat slowly arose, humped his back up high, curled his tail into an impossible position, stuck out each particular hair of his white coat, until he looked like a porcupine, and yawned. Then he closed one eye, and went and rubbed his head sideways against Polly's foot.

"Oh, you lazy Abbott, wake up!" cried Polly, as she caught him in her arms and shook him gently.

"Listen, Abbott! I've something nice to tell you. Tomorrow is Christmas, you know."

Abbott gravely winked. Polly was in the habit of telling her plans to him; and he was a good listener, always agreeing with her.

"Well, now, if you and I were rich, Abbott, we would give each other presents, beautiful presents. People do that at Christmas; did you know it?"

The cat looked inquiringly at her with his bright green eyes. Polly's face was a picture of mock gravity as she said, "I wish I had a present to give you, my poor little cat, but I am so sorry I have none." The cat looked disappointed. "But you shall have an extra saucer of milk tomorrow for breakfast." The cat brightened. "And, Abbott, we'll have a party, you and I, and we'll invite Susie and Mamie Bryce, and Joey Wilkes, and little lame Tim. They are poor little children, Abbott, without any Christmas at all; and you must be a good cat, and play with them, and not go to sleep on the hearth for the whole evening."

Abbott uttered a feeble "Meow!" as protest; but Polly went on:

"We can't have a turkey, it costs too much. Abbott, did you know they always have turkey on Christmas? Yes, and cranberries; but you wouldn't like those: they're sour. We'll have baked beans — they're cheap, you know, and you like them — and an Indian pudding, all baked very nice and brown, with plenty of big, fat raisins in it. And, Abbott, some oysters! Yes, really, just for once. They won't cost much; and you shall have two all to yourself, perhaps three!"

Abbott purred contentedly and settled himself in her lap for another nap; but a gust of air from the window sent Polly in haste to close the forgotten shutters, and the cat concluded it was best to go back to the hearth.

Just as those seven strokes had sounded from Polly's bronze clock, a young man stood on the snowy pavement not many blocks away, hands in his pockets, wondering how he should spend Christmas Eve. He was all alone in the city, too, with not even a cat to cheer him. He had acquaintances, of course — a few — but what were they on Christmas Eve? Some were out of town; and some were in their homes at merrymakings of their own, to which they had not even thought to invite him. He told himself he wouldn't have gone if they had; and he ground his heels into the hard snow, and thought of his mother's cheerful kitchen, with its wide old fireplace and pleasant Christmas odors, the dear father and mother and brother and little sister, even the cat who blinkingly thought over her vanished youth, gazing into the glowing fire. How their faces would brighten if he could walk in upon them now! Indeed, he must stop such thoughts as these. He told himself that he wasn't a baby, to expect always to be at home for Christmas, and to hang up his stocking.

But it was cold, and he could not stand there much longer. Should he go back to his office? No. He had endured that as long as he could for that evening; for John Brewer and his smiling wife, who rented the room just back of his, were having a little tea-drinking, and the peals of merry laughter which came from there every few minutes did not tend to make the young man feel less lonely. He dismissed as quickly the idea that he should go to his dingy little room in the grim boarding-house on High Street. He would call on the gentleman who had left his card that day at the office, with the message that he had some important business matters to talk over with him at his earliest convenience. This would be as good a time as any to call; and the gentleman would be likely to be in his room, as he was a stranger in town. He turned and walked down the little alley, the nearest road to Park Avenue, the Grand Hotel, and the stranger.

Halfway down the alley he discovered he could not recall the name of the man, for he had only glanced at the card hastily as it lay on his table. He fumbled in his pocket for it, so that he might consult it at the next lamp post; but a nearer opportunity offered itself in the shape of Polly Bronson's bright little side window, and he stepped up to it as Polly entered with her bundles. He had just found the right card when he heard the cheery voice calling: "Abbott, come here!" Of course he looked up; and of course, having seen and heard so much, it was not in nature for a lonely man to be in haste to tramp off to make a business call on a stranger. He saw in that fireplace a little of the home cheer of his mother's hearth; he saw in the white cat's face something of the thoughtfulness of the home cat; he saw in the young girl — well, I'm not sure what he saw in her; you'll have to ask him. She was just Polly, you know; something new and bright and beautiful.

Yes, he stood and watched the pretty tableau enacted before him. He let his eyes rove around the little room, and he called it pretty! He did not know the curtains were cheesecloth and the ribbons dyed. He heard every word that Polly said, too — for you remember the window was down from the top — from the presents down to the Indian pudding and the oysters, and wished with all his heart that he was poor little Tim, or somebody who could be invited to that party. Listening? He never thought of such a thing. Indeed, he did not think of anything but the interesting picture and the story that had unfolded itself right before his eyes.

He did recover his senses sufficiently to remember that he was not invisible when Polly came toward the window, and he stepped back into the shadow. There was a sort of blank when the shutters were closed and the cheery room was shut from his view. He did not feel in the least like making that call now. It was scarcely five minutes, and yet he felt that he had some new friends in the city. He had a feeling of pity for the lonely girl; and so in thinking of others, lost sight of his own loneliness.

He very soon discovered that he was standing in a snowbank. Stamping himself out of it, he took his way mechanically to the Grand Hotel, thinking, meanwhile, of what he had seen, reading between the lines of the bit of a story he had been allowed to hear. He was relieved to find that the gentleman of whom he was in search was not in, and he went home with a pleasant little plan taking shape in his brain. It was too bad that the little girl should not have any Christmas present, he thought. What if he should send her one himself? It did not seem exactly the right thing, to send an anonymous present to a young lady who had never seen him; but there certainly could be no harm in sending one to a cat. Nobody ever heard of there being any harm in that.

Very early on Christmas morning, when few in the city were stirring, only the milk wagon or the baker's cart rattling over the frosty stones of the street, and now and then a sleepy clerk taking down shutters and opening doors, he was walking with a brisk step toward a flower store kept by a little old lady of whom he had once or twice bought flowers to send to his mother. He bought a wealth of roses this morning — great yellow Marechal Niels, delicate Safranas only halfway open, and buds of Bon Silines with their wonderful perfume. Then he selected a satin ribbon of faint green tinge for the old lady to fasten them together with, and the whole was put in the prettiest white basket, well wrapped in cotton and white tissue paper, and a card fastened to the handle: "For my friend Abbott, a very Merry Christmas."

Then the young man walked with a smiling face, and calmly deposited the basket on Mr. Samuel Updike's front doorstep and retreated, wishing much that he dared remain and watch the outcome. Polly, who was allowing herself nice long holiday sleeps, slept on with one brown hand under a rosy cheek, and never dreamed that there was a something on her doorstep that would fill her with delight and wonder all that day, and for many days after. But Abbott must have heard a noise, for he shivered a little, opened one eye at the dying fire, wondered why his mistress did not get up, then rolled to the edge of the rug nearest the fire, and went to sleep again.

Polly did wake up by and by, made up

the fire, and got breakfast. After breakfast Abbott sat on the hearth licking his whiskers and washing his paws, and thinking how very nice it was to have an extra saucer of milk, while Polly brushed up the room, opened the windows, and stood the hall door and the front door wide open. There was the basket! Polly's exclamation brought Abbott to the door. He thought it must be another milkman, and he always went to meet the milkman, unless it rained. He sniffed around the basket, and looked as curious as his mistress while she read the card aloud.

"Why, Abbott! It's a Christmas present for you! But who sent it? and what is it? Where did you get a friend that I don't know about? It certainly isn't Mr. or Mrs. Updike, or Peter Kelly, or the milkman; and I'm sure I don't know who else knows you. O Abbott, I wish you could talk!"

Abbott tried to let her know by eyes and ears, as well as a cat can, that if he could talk he could give her no information on the subject.

"Let's open it, Abbott."

Thereupon the cat and basket were transferred to the sofa. Amid many exclamations the roses came to light, filling the little room with their elegant fragrance.

Polly caught the cat up, and kissed the very tip of his pink ear. It was dreadful, I know; but then Polly was very happy, and she had no one else to kiss.

"You dear cat! You shall invite your friend to the party, so you shall, if you will give the invitation."

Perhaps Abbott understood, for he went to the door and sat looking out. Presently he walked down the steps and over the snowy path, putting each paw down carefully, lest it might get too much mixed with the snow. When he reached the gate he gave one spring to the top of the gatepost, and paused a moment, looking up and down the street, and then, seeming to decide which way he would go, sprang down, and trotted off as though he had business that would require haste.

Polly talked to everything that morning while she worked. She called to Abbott at the door that he should wear the green ribbon to the party; and he looked back and winked assent as he put the first velvet paw into the snow. She told the vases that they were dear, beautiful things, and she was glad at last that there was something for them to hold, and she hoped they would keep them very carefully a long time. Polly worked fast, and was soon ready to go out

to do her marketing and give her invitations. She decided to have her party at
night; because Mamie Bryce had to go
down on Sycamore Street and take care of
Mrs. Dobell's baby, while Mrs. Dobell
went to a dinner party, and she could not
get back until four o'clock. So Polly told
them all to come at five; and their eyes
shone brightly as they promised.

It was beginning to grow dark. Little
flurries of snow filled the air. The young
man — Porter Mason was his name —
hurried along the street, hands in his pockets, collar turned up, and hat drawn over
his eyes. He had been away off to the other
end of the city on some good errand or
other; was cold and tired and hungry, and
it was still a long walk home. He was wondering if he should dare to venture around
to that alley again when it grew quite dark;
if the window blinds would be open; if he
should see the roses anywhere; and if the
party would be over. In a lull between the
chime of sleigh bells came a faint "Meow!"
and he looked sharply around. The
"Meow-ow-ow-ow!" came more distinctly
now; and soon just ahead of him he spied a
weary white form moving dejectedly
through the fast-falling snow. He stooped
and picked it up, brushing the snow off,

and holding it up to the light of a near street lamp.

"I believe you are the very cat!" he said, speaking aloud. "But how in the world did you get here? Is your name Abbott?"

"Meow!" said the cat.

"All right, then; you're my friend. Jump right in here and make yourself comfortable." He opened his big overcoat, and tucked the cat snugly in. "I shouldn't wonder if I had my invitation, after all," he told himself as he went on briskly.

Within Polly Bronson's cheery room all was not as serene as might have been. The little party had assembled, and were sitting on the edges of their chairs, undergoing the first embarrassment of arrival; but there was a shadow besides embarrassment over them. The trouble was that two of them were missing. The one was the guest little Tim, and the other was the host himself, Abbott. Tim could not come, because his father was too drunk to carry him, and the streets were too slippery to trust him with his little crutch. His mother would have brought him, for it was his first bit of pleasure for many a day; but she, poor soul, was on her back, scarcely able to wait upon herself. Nobody knew what had become of Abbott.

That is the way matters stood when Porter Mason rang the bell of the Updike house, which so startled Susie and Mamie Bryce and Joey Wilkes that they all huddled together on one chair, like so many frightened peas in a pan when the pan is suddenly tipped up. Mr. Mason had gone straight to the little lane side window, and found the shutters closed. Now what should he do? Would it be safe to risk a peep in at the front window? Suppose the real Abbott were inside, snug and warm by the fire? How foolish he would feel appearing at the door of a strange young lady, in the dark of a snowy night, and saying, "Have you lost a cat, madam?" without giving a reason for supposing that she had a cat.

He stood in the snowbank again and thought, and kitty purred under his warm coat. He might say that he had once, when passing, seen a cat there. It wasn't in the least likely that the young lady would question him as to the circumstances under which he had seen the cat, and she would in all probability suppose him to have seen it on the doorstep. He concluded to risk this statement, and so boldly rang the bell.

Polly hurried to the door. She was not in the habit of having evening callers. The door, being opened, let in such a whirl-wind of snowflakes that Polly could distinguish nothing in the gathering darkness save the tall form of a man powdered with snow from head to foot. He was taking off his hat and saying in a pleasant voice, "Have you lost a cat?" As he said it he cast an anxious glance through the half-open door to the glowing fireplace, and was relieved to see no cat there.

"Oh, yes!" her senses having come back to her. "Won't you come in? Do you know where he is?"

"I found one on the street; and, remembering to have seen one at this house, I brought it here."

He was unbuttoning his coat now, and handed Abbott, warm and somewhat damp, to his mistress.

"Oh, thank you so much!" she said as she took him. "I'm so glad to get him back. I was troubled about him when it began to snow so hard. I was afraid he was lost."

She paused and looked up. Abbott's rescuer looked very cold and blue as he stood there in the chilly hall. Perhaps he had come out of his way to bring the cat, she thought. He had a chilly feeling at his heart too; he began to think that it was time he should say, "You're quite welcome;

good-evening," and bow himself out, and go to his cold, dingy room. He seemed to see the supper to which he would presently be called, remnants of the departed dinner. He glanced again into the cheery room, and then was about to bow his good-evening, when Polly's voice interrupted — "Won't you come in to the fire and get warm? You must be very cold."

Polly never thought of being afraid to ask a stranger in. She was never afraid of anything. She was twenty-two, and had taken care of herself for nearly five years, and she felt as if nothing in the world could harm her. Then there were the children; and she had a secure sense of Peter Kelly in his back chamber over the kitchen. Besides, had not this stranger done her a kindness; and did she not owe something to him? And he had kind eyes, and a gentle hand with the kitten. There are always reasons enough when a bright girl does anything.

But she was surprised when, instead of saying, "No, I thank you," he hesitated, and said, "May I?"

Polly, with glowing cheeks, ushered her caller into the bright room, and seated him in the rocking chair, hardly knowing what to make of him, or what to do with him when she got him there. But the children helped her with their gleeful exclamations over the lost-and-found cat. Abbott, however, slipped from their caressing hands, and retired to the hearth to bathe. He was a neat cat, and did not like to appear before company with his white coat all stiff and rough.

"Where did you say you found him?" questioned Polly. Mr. Mason did not say, but launched into a full description of Abbott's pitiful cries and forlorn appearance, until the question was forgotten in a merry round of laughter, in which Polly joined, in spite of herself, although she had determined to be very dignified.

"Oh!" cried Susie when the laughter had somewhat subsided, "wouldn't we be having just a lovely time if Tim were only here."

"Yes," said Mamie, the laughter all sobered out of her face. "He stood at the top of the stairs, and cried and cried when we came down." And even stout little Joey Wilkes said it was "just too awful mean for anything."

"And who is Tim?" asked the strange visitor, as soon as there was any chance for him to speak.

The children burst into full explanation of the case, all together of course, and it was some time before he could understand. Even then he was left in doubt as to whether more sorrow had been felt for Abbott, or for little Tim with his drunken father.

He arose at last, and turned to Polly, "Having brought back one of the missing guests, it becomes needful that I should complete my good work, and bring the other. It would be a pity to have the perfection of this party spoiled by the shadow of an absent guest. Can you direct me where to find this boy?"

He buttoned up his coat, and the children danced for joy and clapped their hands, crying, "Goody, goody!"

Polly's face was beaming all over with a pleased surprise; but she tried to draw up her slipping cloak of dignity, and say, "Oh, no! You really must not go to that trouble for us this stormy night."

Mr. Mason, however, would listen to no such talk, and obtained the desired information. He turned to go, then stopped, fumbling in his pockets; but as no card was to be found, he produced a bit of folded pasteboard, saying, "I have no card with me, but will this do as well? My name is the fourth one on the list of leaders, and when I come back we'll get Tim to introduce us."

The well-known letters "Y. P. S. C. E." met her eyes from the cover of the card, and below, "Hartford Square Church." A little smile played over her face. She need not be quite so careful now that she knew so much about him. Turning to the next page, she ran over the list of leaders and their subjects, especially the fourth one. She laid the card on the shelf, and went back to her oil stove. The pudding was just taking on the last delicate shades of brown, and needed watching. She hastened to set her table, putting one more plate on; for, she told herself, she supposed that young man must be invited to supper, after he had taken so much trouble for them. Then she thought of Peter Kelly.

Now, Peter was of that nondescript age when one does not know what to call him. It seemed strange to designate him as a young man; and yet he was not a boy, nor an old man, nor even a middle-aged man. Yes, he certainly must be a young man; but it seemed so odd to call him that. He had colorless hair and expressionless eyes. The world had not used him badly; indeed, it had not used him much at all either way, and he had not used it; therefore he had no identity with it. Peter was connected with the Hartford Square Church; that is, he swept the floors and looked after the rooms — was, in short, janitor. Remembering this, she filled a plate with some baked beans and one slice of the delicate toast that stood ready for the hot oysters, and pouring a cup of steaming coffee, she went with swift steps to the back chamber, and knocked.

The front legs of Peter's chair came to the floor with a bang, and he sat with his mouth wide open, staring at the door, after giving his gruff, "Come in."

Polly entered, setting down her burden and saying rapidly, "I've brought you some of my baked beans; they're hot, and I thought you might like them, Peter."

She never knew what sort of thanks he stammered out. She was busy thinking how she should put her question.

"Peter, do you know any one at the Hartford Square Church by the name of Mason?"

This was as near the name as she would come. She would not have dared so much if he had been like some people; but talking to Peter was much like talking to Abbott. He would never put two and two together, or wonder why she had asked such a question.

"Wal, yas," said Peter, diverted from his astonishment; "thar's two on 'em. Thar's John — he's a carpenter; an' thar's Porter — he's a law'er. I reckon you mean him. Is he tall an' han'some? great big eyes an' black hair, an' allus a good word said jes so's to help most?"

"I think he must be the gentleman I have met," said Polly demurely.

"Wal, he's a mighty nice feller; give me a ticket to a church supper th' other evenin'. He's awful smart, too, an' good. They do say he wouldn't have nothin' to do with a case Judge Granger give him, cause he thought it wa'n't right; an' he ain't rich, neither. But you'd just ought to hear him pray! Thar's allus a big meetin' up to the C.E. when he leads."

Polly had all the information she wanted now, and made haste to get away, amid a shower of rough thanks from Peter. She went gleefully to her room, and found the children so busy with a picture book that they had scarcely noticed her absence. So she knelt by the fireplace and stroked Abbott. Now that he was dry and smooth, Polly tied the rich green ribbon around his neck, much to the delight of the children. She stuck a Safrana bud in the bow, and set him upon the stool. There he sat, the

329

long ends of shining satin reaching to his toes, holding his chin very high, either from the choking sensation of the broad ribbon, or pride in his rich apparel; probably pride, for he seemed quite contented, and sat purring at the children with his eyes half closed.

Porter Mason, with happy Tim mounted on his shoulder, came to a sudden halt before a large fruit store.

"Tim, would you like to take Miss Bronson a Christmas present?" he asked.

They had been talking of her all the way along, and Tim had said he loved her next best to his mother in all the world. They were pretty well acquainted by this time, so Tim answered, "You just bet! Wouldn't I, though?"

"All right. We'll go in here, and you shall choose what it shall be."

It almost took Tim's breath away to see so many good things together; but after grave consideration he pointed to a box of great white California grapes. You might have thought Mr. Mason extravagant for a man who "wasn't rich" if you'd heard his order to the clerk; but little Tim was very happy, and his companion looked none the less so.

"Well, Miss Bronson," said Mr. Mason,

after they were fairly in, and Tim had presented his gift, "is the courier to be allowed to stay to the party, or must I go outside and paw the pavement until my services are needed again? Or I might go off and come back at a certain hour?"

What could Polly do but give him a gracious invitation?

So he took his coat and hat to the hall, and made himself quite at home, telling the children stories, and giving them such a wonderful time, while Polly cooked the oysters, that they forgot how hungry they were. They had a great time getting seated at the table. Polly actually ventured to borrow four of Mrs. Updike's best splint-bottomed kitchen chairs, and they all went after them except Tim and Abbott, who sat and smiled at one another while they were gone. But they were seated at last, and then came a moment Polly was not altogether prepared for. She had meant to ask a blessing. She always did when by herself, and she wanted not to leave God out before these children, and on Christmas night; but here was this stranger. Could she ask him?

Polly's daring spirit came uppermost. She looked up and said quietly, "Will you ask a blessing?"

Then what a light of pleasure and surprise rushed into the eyes that met hers. He bowed his head, and his few earnest, clear-spoken words to God astonished the children more than his stories had done. They were evidently not used to this.

While Polly was pouring out coffee, Mr. Mason questioned the children, and found they knew almost nothing at all about Christmas; so he promised to tell them the true story of it after tea, and they gave themselves up to the delights of their plates.

"Miss Bronson promised to sing some too," said Susie Bryce, with her mouth full of beans. Now, Polly did not intend to keep that promise, with the stranger there to listen; so she passed him the sugar, and asked Tim if he would have some more oysters. The Indian pudding was hailed with joy, and pronounced by Mr. Mason "just as good as his mother's." Then they finished off with some of those luscious grapes. They were such a treat to Polly, and to the children something wonderful. Abbott had his three oysters, and enjoyed them as much as anybody.

After supper, while Polly, was clearing off the table, the children had their story. Polly, going about her work very softly, that she might lose none of it, told herself that she did not wonder that they liked to come to meeting when he led, if he talked like that. When she had finished she sat down very quietly, but the story was just closing, and Mr. Mason turned to her and said, "Now may we have the song, Miss Bronson?"

Polly did not wish, did not intend, to sing to him. She had "No" written all over her pretty, flushed face, despite the children's eager pleadings, until Mr. Mason said, "I think I shall have to go out and stand in the snow, after all, for I don't want the children to lose their pleasure because of me."

Polly somehow had to sing then; and though her voice trembled some, it was sweet and clear as she sang:

"*Little stars that twinkle in the heavens blue,*
I have often wondered if you ever knew
How there rose one like you, leading wise old men
From the east, through Judah, down to Bethlehem?

Did you watch the Savior all those years of strife?

*Did you know for sinners, how he gave
  his life?
Little stars that twinkle in the heavens blue,
All you saw of Jesus, how I wish I knew."*

Then Polly stopped; and she would not
sing again for all their coaxing, for she had
been too conscious of those eyes that had
watched her so closely during the singing
to try again. So she started some games,
and they had a frolic until the clock on the
mantel warned them that it was getting
late, and Mr. Mason told little Tim it was
time for his carriage to take him home.
The children sighed that the happy time
was over. Tim was given some of the
grapes and a rosebud or two for his sick
mother. Polly bundled him up, and gave
each of the children a rose, and then they
were ready to go.

Mr. Mason gravely walked up to the fire,
where weary Abbott, in spite of his ele-
gance, had succumbed to the warmth and
the remembrance of a delicious supper,
and had gone to sleep. But he was a polite
cat, and as Mr. Mason came up, let him
shake hands, or paws, with him.

Tim was mounted once more on his
shoulder; Polly's hand was taken for just a
second, and — "I have enjoyed it all so

much; might I come again soon, and make a party call?"

Of course she had to say yes; and then, with Susie and Mamie just behind, and Joey Wilkes scudding on ahead, they started out into the snow, and the party was ended.

Yes, he came very soon to make the call; and then he wanted to come again and again, until it grew to be a settled thing for him to run in once or twice a week with a bit of a poem for her to read, or a book to talk over. In those days she had roses sent to her, instead of to her cat; she was taken out to Sunday evening meetings quite often, and now and then to a concert or a lecture. Abbott was left at home, which he did not like after having been alone all day. As spring came on there were violets and anemones, and once a lovely ride to the woods on a Saturday afternoon. Then a note came from the mother of a former pupil, saying that her little daughter was very sick, could not live long, and wanted to have her dear Miss Bronson with her, which the doctor said would help. Would she come to them as soon as possible?

Polly sighed, packed away her bronze clock and marble vases, packed up the things she must take with her, waited a

whole day hoping somebody would call —
then gave Abbott into the keeping of a
quaint new neighbor. She gave special directions to Mrs. Updike to say to whoever
called that she had been summoned to a
sick friend and would probably be back
soon, and went.

It was not a long journey, fifty miles or
so, and the little pupil was very glad to see
her. She grew no better as the days went
by. It soon became evident that Polly could
not be spared, for Bessie was not happy a
moment unless her teacher was by her
side. The mother was an invalid herself,
who made her little girl worse by her mel-
ancholy speeches; so, although Polly was
longing to be at home, she did not feel as if
she ought to go. She stayed, and Bessie
grew day by day weaker, but lingered on
until the summer was drawing near its
close, and the winter school term was
about to begin; then she slipped into
heaven, leaving Polly, who had made the
way bright for her, almost worn out with
loss of sleep and confinement to the sick
room. She hurried home to begin school
life again. She unpacked the clock and
vases, and reestablished Abbott, who
walked round and round her, purring and
rubbing his head against her, trying as best

he could to tell that he did not like boarding, and was glad to be at home again. When Polly received the key of her room, and asked if there had been anyone to call, she gained only a sentence about a tall man who "kep' a coming"; and that was all the news of home she had.

Porter Mason had been very lonely after Polly left. He had called many times to see her; but Mrs. Updike never knew her address, and now, just as Polly had come home, he had been called away on business. When he finally reached home he found such a quantity of matters awaiting his attention that he had no time to think of doing anything for pleasure. So it happened that Polly had been at home for three weeks without once having seen Mr. Mason.

One evening she took Abbott in her arms and went to the front door. The air was chilly and hazy, as late September is apt to be. The stars were not nearly as bright as usual. They had no sparkle. They looked as if they had all gone away to spend the evening, and had left only a dim light in the window. It was lonesome and cold. She shivered, and dropped a few tears on Abbott's thick coat. She did not hear the brisk steps coming down the street as she went in and shut the door; but they came on, right to Polly's bright little window, which had been so dark for many a day when those same steps had sounded down the street. And when Mr. Mason came in he took Polly's two hands in his own and held them — Abbott had his back turned, looking into the fire — and when he had made her quite comfortable on the sofa, he sat down beside her, and told her something; but we must not hear it. If you have heard such words yourself, you understand; if you have not, wait until your turn comes to know.

What did Polly say? Why, she said it to Mr. Mason; and no one heard, not even Abbott, for he was asleep, and Mr. Mason never told.

They both went to the cheerful home among the hills to spend their next holidays, and make glad the hearts of the dear father and mother and brother and little sister and the other cat. Abbott, much to his disgust, was obliged to spend his holidays with the quaint little neighbor; and when his mistress came back she took him to another part of the town to live, where the familiar objects were all about him. There was a rug that he always lay on, crocheted out of strips of silk; and the yellow stripes were the yellow ribbons that used to hold back the cheesecloth curtains. He thought it rather queer that Polly never went to school anymore, and that the tall stranger stayed all the time now; but he liked him and so it was all right. He had all the beefsteak and milk and oysters he wanted, and could wear a green ribbon and rosebuds any day if he chose — so he told the cats of the neighborhood.

And so the old room has seen the story; has helped it along, as it has helped many before, and stands again waiting, all alone, except for the big black spider who is hanging her delicate draperies in all the corners. It waits for someone to enter and bring life and beauty to it again.

The employees of Thorndike Press hope you have enjoyed this Large Print book. All our Large Print titles are designed for easy reading, and all our books are made to last. Other Thorndike Press Large Print books are available at your library, through selected bookstores, or directly from us.

For information about titles, please call:

(800) 257-5157

To share your comments, please write:

Publisher
Thorndike Press
P.O. Box 159
Thorndike, Maine 04986